CW01018883

The Balaclava Brigade Victorious

Written and Illustrated by

Roland Bond

authorHOUSE®

AuthorHouse™ UK Ltd.
500 Avebury Boulevard
Central Milton Keynes, MK9 2BE
www.authorhouse.co.uk
Phone: 08001974150

First published by AuthorHouse 2/16/2009

ISBN: 978-1-4389-2010-8 (sc)

Printed in the United States of America
Bloomington, Indiana

This book is printed on acid-free paper.

This book is dedicated to the members of that amusing and adventurous band of village children whose company and friendship the author was privileged to enjoy during his World War II evacuation.

Chapter 1

Back at School

"Come here, boy!" bellowed a loud voice.

It was Friday afternoon, and crowds of noisy children were crossing the playground at Brinton National School. Everyone was excited because we had completed our first week back at school after the long summer holidays. My friend, Georgie, and I were making our way to the ramshackle old bus which was waiting outside the school gates. Since we lived in the neighbouring village we had to travel to and from school by bus each day.

"I said come here!" the stern voice yelled once more.

We turned quickly to see Mr. Hardcastle, our headmaster, standing in the school doorway. The playground had suddenly fallen still and silent. Mr. Hardcastle was a tall upright man, a hugely impressive figure with steel grey hair and a thin moustache.

The Head's commanding voice rang out again even more loudly.

"You, boy! I said come here!"

All the children were rooted to the spot, totally motionless like marble statues.

Intense anger glared out from the Head's face, and his tone of voice conveyed extreme displeasure. His eyes blazed across the playground, but his finger which was waving around aimlessly did not appear to be pointing at anyone in particular. Mr. Hardcastle had been an army officer in the blood-soaked trenches of the First World War where he had lost an eye, which had been replaced with a glass one. A puzzled expression stared out from every child's face. The problem was that his two eyes always seemed to be looking in different directions, and therefore it was impossible to decide who he was actually looking at. Who was in trouble this time? That was the question!

It was now September 1940, and our country had been at war with Hitler's Germany for exactly one year. I had been evacuated away from my Birmingham home to the small Midland coal-mining village of Stretton-on-the-Hill. During the long summer holidays my friends and I had formed ourselves into the Balaclava Brigade, a military style unit with a brigade headquarters in an old pigsty in Georgie's back garden.

"You!" the Head yelled again impatiently, his outstretched finger waving around in the air like a young tree in a blustery wind. "I said, 'Come here!' Did you not hear me?"

Half a dozen guilty-looking boys pointed at themselves and chorused, "Me sir?"

"That boy there! The one with the untidy hair and the wrinkled socks around his ankles! Come here immediately!" Mr. Hardcastle bawled.

This time two boys responded, "Me, sir?"

The Head tried again.

"I mean that boy with filthy knees and the enormous hole in the front of his jumper."

When he was angry Mr. Hardcastle would never address a child by name. It was always, "You boy!" or "That girl there!" It was almost as if he thought that addressing a child by name under such circumstances would be interpreted as a sign of friendliness.

My parents had assured me that, if I went to live in a country village, I would be safe from the German bombers which had started to attack our ports and cities. During the first year of my evacuation I had lived with an evil old witch of a woman called Wilma Jones, before moving to live in the cottage next door with my best friend, Georgie Millward, his younger brother, Jimmy, and their parents.

"Come here!" the Head bellowed again, for he was clearly losing patience.

Georgie and I were now in no doubt whom Mr. Hardcastle wanted to talk to.

"D'you mean me, sir," piped up a small untidy-looking boy.

It was Baz, an unruly scruffy little Stretton lad with a shock of untidy blonde hair. He was a lance-corporal in our Balaclava Brigade.

"Yes boy, I mean *you*. Come here, this instant!"

Georgie and I were not surprised that Baz was the object of Mr. Hardcastle's displeasure. Our little lance-corporal was always getting into trouble, but I could not help wondering what he had been up to this time. I looked again at the furious expression on Mr. Hardcastle's face. Leaning towards Georgie I whispered in his ear.

"I wouldn't like to be in Baz's boots right now."

"Nor me," answered my friend. "Mr. Hardcastle looks really mad. I reckon Baz is in loads of trouble this time!"

Chapter 2

Double Trouble for Baz

"Come on, boy!" shouted the irate Head. "I haven't got all day!"

Baz lowered his tousled head and slouched back to Mr. Hardcastle, dragging his feet across the tarmac. His long matted blonde hair hung over his eyes like a grubby worn-out curtain. His grimy face looked confused. A gaping hole dominated the front of his jumper, and his socks lay collapsed and crumpled above a pair of scuffed muddy boots.

A second boy now emerged from behind Mr. Hardcastle. He was a thin weasel-faced lad with drooping shoulders and mousey hair. This was Archie Fraser, who had recently arrived in our village with his mum and his elder sister, because they had been bombed out of their London home. He was the grandson of Wilma Jones, that horrible old woman who had made my life such a misery when I was billeted with her and her henpecked husband, Cyril.

"And what were you doing at playtime this afternoon, may I ask?" demanded the incensed Head, his right hand pointing at our untidy little comrade, and the other resting in a kindly fashion upon Archie Fraser's shoulder.

"I dain't do nothin', Mr. 'Ardcastle," answered Baz, staring blankly at his accuser.

"I dain't do nothin'!" repeated the headmaster. "I dain't do nothin'! What do you mean, I dain't do nothin'?"

"I dain't, Mr. 'Ardcastle," insisted Baz. "I dain't do nothin'!"

"There is no such word as 'dain't' and it should be 'anything' not 'nothing'. Repeat after me, boy, 'I did not do anything'."

Gazing at the ground, Baz repeated the Head's words hesitantly as if he was speaking an unfamiliar foreign language. Mr. Hardcastle stared at his young pupil, searching the boy's face for the slightest sign that he may not be telling the truth. Baz glanced up nervously into the tall man's face which was oozing with mistrust.

"But I dain't do nothin', sir," Baz insisted again with even greater conviction.

The Head took a sharp intake of breath and shook his head before continuing.

"This boy tells me that you have ripped the neck of his jumper," reported Mr. Hardcastle, pointing to Archie Fraser. "Is that true?"

"Yes, Mr. 'Ardcastle," admitted Baz quietly.

"And would you mind explaining why you have ripped his jumper?"

"'Cus he ripped mine, Mr. 'Ardcastle," replied Baz in a quavering voice.

"No I didn't," protested the weasel-faced lad.

"Yes you did!" insisted Baz, pointing in a deliberate manner at the huge hole in the front of his jumper.

"His jumper has been like that for ages, sir," replied the other boy.

"Yeah, but you made it much worser," protested Baz loudly.

"Much worser!" bellowed the flustered Mr. Hardcastle. "You mean he made it worse!"

"Yes Mr. 'Ardcastle, 'e made it much worser."

The tall man made a conscious effort to compose himself before beginning again in a more gentle tone.

"Now let us try to get to the bottom of this matter. Who started it?"

"He did," cried both boys, each pointing an accusing finger at the other.

Mr. Hardcastle was unimpressed. His face was fiery red, his fists were clenched tightly and his thin moustache was twitching visibly.

"I would like *you* to tell me how it all started," he said, turning towards Wilma Jones's grandson.

Prodding an index finger towards Baz, Archie Fraser started to recount his side of the story.

"He keeps looking at my work in class, sir, and laughing at it. Today I was drawing this picture of a witch in the forest and he said that it was my grandma."

"Well, 'e said things about me gran," replied Baz in self defence, "and 'e said it first, before I said it to 'im."

"Right, I have heard enough! I will see both of you first thing on Monday morning, as soon as you get to school. But I warn you, I will not have you fighting and squabbling like this. And I certainly will not tolerate you tearing each others' clothes. There is a war on! Clothes cost a lot of money and they are in short supply. They don't grow on trees, you know. Do you understand?"

"Yes, Mr. 'Ardcastle," muttered Baz.

"Yes, sir," repeated Archie Fraser.

Before continuing, the headmaster looked Baz up and down for several seconds in the manner of an undertaker sizing someone up for a coffin.

"Right! Archibald Fraser, you may go to catch your bus now, but I want a word with you, young man," and he grabbed hold of Baz very firmly by the shoulder.

By this time all the children had melted away, either to walk home or to catch the bus from outside the school gates, but Georgie and I had remained behind to see what was going to happen. After all, Baz was a lance-corporal in our Balaclava Brigade. We had all sworn an oath to look after one another in times of trouble, and we had adopted 'All for one and one for all' as our brigade motto. There was no way that we could go home and abandon Baz in his hour of need

The tall headmaster bent forward and peered into Baz's grimy and confused face.

"Now boy," he began, "whenever I walk into your classroom you always seem to be standing in the corner facing the wall. Is that not so?"

"Yes, Mr. 'Ardcastle," replied Baz, his eyes staring down at the playground.

"When I entered your classroom this week I noticed that you had been told to stand in the corner once again. I believe Mrs. Jolly had been trying to encourage the class to write longer sentences. Is that not so, boy?"

"Yes, Mr. 'Ardcastle," Baz answered, still looking down.

"And when she asked what was meant by 'a longer sentence' I understand you put your hand up."

"Yes Mr. 'Ardcastle," was the inevitable response.

"And what did you say in reply to her question?"

Baz glanced up into the tall man's face and replied confidently, "I said 'five years', Mr. 'Ardcastle, 'cus that's what me Uncle Alfie got for selling stuff on the Black Market."

Mr. Hardcastle stood up straight, sighed deeply, wrung his hands together and cast his eyes skywards. The despairing headmaster aimed another withering look at his wayward young pupil before bending forward once more.

"Why is it that you are always getting into trouble?" he asked.

Baz hung his shaggy head and stared silently at the toe caps of his scuffed boots.

"I will tell you why! It is because you are constantly misbehaving. On the first day back at school after the summer holiday, you broke a window in the classroom."

"But I never meant to, Mr. 'Ardcastle," replied Baz innocently.

"What do you mean, boy, you 'never meant to'?"

"I never meant to bust the window. It were Archie Fraser's fault."

"And why was it Archie Fraser's fault?"

"Well, I chucked me biggest and best conker at 'im, an' if 'e 'adn't 'ave ducked, me conker wouldn't 'ave busted the window," argued Baz. "That conker were a 'forty-niner'."

"But it most definitely *was* your fault. *You* were the person who threw that conker. You are not allowed to throw things at one another in this school. You all know that! If you had hit Archibald Fraser in the eye with your 'forty-niner' you could have blinded him. Furthermore, you seem to forget that there is a war on. Broken windows cannot be repaired easily these days."

Baz hung his shaggy head once more.

There were several seconds of total silence while Mr. Hardcastle fixed Baz with another long steely-eyed stare. Then he continued.

"The story of your misdeeds, young man, would fill several large volumes. Last term you thought it would be an excellent idea to bring a surprise to school for your teacher. A surprise it most certainly was! When that huge frog jumped out of her respirator box during gas mask practice the poor lady fainted on the floor. It took us ten minutes to catch the frog and a quarter of an hour to bring Miss Forrester around! Furthermore, when your class went on a nature walk in the woods you thought it would be a marvellous idea to put a gigantic worm down the back of Matilda Ford's dress. If I remember correctly the nature walk had to be abandoned because Matilda would not stop howling with that worm wriggling around in the middle of her back. I also recall an incident when you placed a massive hairy spider on top of Lucy Higginbothom's desk. Your foolish action caused half a dozen girls to dash to the front of the classroom shrieking and screaming hysterically. Chairs went clattering over and books went flying across the classroom. It caused more panic than a sudden air-raid by the entire German air force. I could go on recounting your misdemeanours, boy," continued the Head, wagging his finger in front of Baz's nose.

The untidy pupil hung his head once more and fidgeted uncomfortably.

"If there are any further incidents this term I shall be sending for your mother and father. You had better watch your step, my boy, and pull your socks up!"

"Yes, Mr. 'Ardcastle," answered Baz in a broken voice, and on upon hearing the words 'pull your socks up', he bent over and hauled up first one wrinkled sock and then the other.

"And don't forget. I shall want to see you first thing on Monday morning outside my room. And I suggest that you wash your hands, face and knees before you present yourself at my door again. And more importantly, you would look a great deal tidier if you had some of that ridiculous hair chopped off. See to it, boy!"

Having issued his instructions, Mr. Hardcastle turned on his heels abruptly and marched smartly into school. Georgie and I waited for our headmaster to disappear inside the building, and then we walked across to where Baz was standing.

"Hey, Baz!" I said. "What's happened this time?"

"Archie Fraser told 'im that I ripped 'is jumper but it were 'is fault. 'E started it. And now 'e's got me into trouble again."

Although he was well known for being wild and unruly, Baz had a keen sense of justice. If he knew that he had done something wrong, he would accept his punishment without complaint. But he hated to bear the blame for any incident when he was convinced that someone else was more at fault. As we walked home from school through the woods (for we had missed the bus) there was only one topic of conversation – Archie Fraser.

When we finally reached the middle of our village, we were very concerned about the sight which met our eyes. Standing on the pavement outside her front gate was that evil old woman, Wilma Jones, attired in a long floral pinafore apron. Her grandson Archie was standing beside her. Anger was etched all over the old witch's horrible face, and her right arm was dangling protectively over Archie's shoulder. I knew that Baz had got himself into loads of bother at school with Mr. Hardcastle but, when I looked at Wilma's contorted face, I could not help thinking that his troubles for the day were only just beginning!

Chapter 3

Wilma's Threat

We had to walk past Wilma's cottage to reach home so there was no way of avoiding her. As we tried to pass by, she stepped in front of us, barring our way. The look on her face was both unpleasant and threatening. Leaning forward, she glared at us. Her sunken cheeks were glowing bright red, her mouth was slightly open and her large stained teeth looked like the moss-covered gravestones in Brinton churchyard. Still clutching his grandmother's hand, Archie was grinning unattractively.

"That's him!" Archie exclaimed, his right hand pointing directly at Baz.

"What have you been doing to my Archie at school?" screamed Wilma, her tall thin frame stooping forward towards our little lance-corporal.

"'E started it all," responded Baz defensively.

"No I didn't gran. Honest! It was him. He called you a witch. And he said you keep a flying broomstick in your wash house."

"No I never! I never said nothin' about a broomstick!" protested Baz.

"Yes you did! And he said that you fly all round the village at night, casting horrible spells on people."

"I never!" insisted Baz, with a look of utter disbelief.

Georgie and I knew that Baz was not averse to telling the odd lie or two, but we could always tell when he was being honest. This time, without a shadow of a doubt, Baz was telling the truth.

Archie looked up at his grandma with huge wide eyes before continuing.

"And he said that you've got a big iron pot hanging over the fire in your living room, grandma, and that you put snakes and toads and lizards and bats' wings into it, and then you boil them all up to make a special brew for casting spells on people, grandma."

This boy certainly had a vivid imagination! What Archie was saying sounded like something straight out of a story which he had been writing in the classroom. Wilma was fuming, her face was beetroot red and her fierce eyes were burning into Baz like streaks of forked lightening. Her long bony fingers had tightened on Archie's shoulder. As she bent her willowy frame towards Baz once more she glowered into his face, her beak-like nose almost touching his cheek. Her long index finger was prodding him fiercely in the chest.

"On Monday morning I'm going up to that school," she hissed threateningly between her tombstone teeth. "Then we'll see what the headmaster has to say about all this."

Next she turned to face Georgie and me.

"And I expect you two are mixed up in this as well, causing trouble as usual. I shall report all of you to the headmaster on Monday morning."

She grabbed her grandson's hand and turned away. As she led Archie towards her front gate, she bent down and muttered a few consoling words into his ear.

Georgie and I were totally bewildered.

"Why is she going to report us to Mr. Hardcastle," I muttered. "It was nothing to do with us."

"Probably Archie wants to get us into trouble as well," replied Georgie.

"Well I know Wilma doesn't like me," I said. "She was always horrible to me when I was living with her and Cyril. She only kept me there so that she could use my ration book."

"I dain't say nothin' about broomsticks and spells and cookin' pots, 'onest," insisted Baz. "Anyway, 'e were the one what started it."

"Don't you worry, Baz," said Georgie. "The Balaclava Brigade will deal with Archie Fraser."

"Yes, that little liar may have won the opening battle," I murmured. "But one thing's for sure - the Balaclava Brigade is definitely going to win the war!"

Chapter 4

A New Recruit

The next day was Saturday and we had the whole weekend to ourselves. When we had finished breakfast, Jimmy pulled on his favourite multi-coloured striped jumper and ran into the yard with a hop and a skip. He was unable to bend his right knee because it had been damaged in a road accident. Georgie grabbed a piece of crusty bread from the table, and popped it into his mouth. Then the three of us wandered round to the front of the cottage where we stood on the pavement beside the main road which ran through our village.

"Hello! What are you doing?" yelled a shrill voice from the other side of the road.

I glanced up. A girl was standing on the pavement opposite, and she was staring at us. I guessed that she was about 10 years old, the same age as Georgie and me. She was tall, slim and very pretty, with beautiful long black hair, tied in a pony tail.

"We're waiting for the rest of our brigade to come out," answered Georgie.

"Ooh! Can I join your brigade?" she asked, her dark eyes glinting in the strong sunlight.

Georgie and I glanced at one another. Who on earth was this girl? Where had she come from? We had never seen *her* before.

"Well, only kids who live in Stretton can join our brigade," I shouted.

The girl skipped across the road to join us outside the Millwards' cottage.

"But I live in Stretton now," she said, looking at each of us in turn. "My name is Rose but all my friends call me Rosie. You can call me Rosie if you like! I've been sent to live here because of the bombing. My dad's a sergeant-major in the army and my mum works at the BSA factory, making machine gun bullets for the war."

"You must come from Birmingham then," I said. "I'm an evacuee as well and I come from Birmingham. My name's Tommy."

"Which part do you come from?" she asked.

"My home's in Erdington, not far from Fort Dunlop," I answered. "Where do you live?"

"I live in Small Heath near the factory where my mum works. What are *your* names?" she inquired, looking at my two friends.

"My name's Georgie and this is my brother, Jimmy."

She smiled at both of them.

"How about it then? Can I join your brigade?" she asked once more.

"But our brigade is just like a proper army," replied Jimmy.

"Yes, we've got officers and a sergeant and corporals and things like that," added Georgie.

"Well, girls can join the army," Rosie replied, "because my cousin, Dorothy, has joined the A.T.S."

"What's the A.T.S.?" asked Jimmy.

"It's called the Auxiliary Territorial Service - the part of the army that women go into when they join up," replied Rosie

"Well, what does your cousin do in the A.T.S.?" I asked.

"She fires an anti-aircraft gun. She's shot down three German planes already," Rosie answered proudly. "Can I join your brigade, please?"

I was very impressed to hear the news about her cousin, Dorothy.

"You have to be able to throw things and aim properly to be a member of the Balaclava Brigade," Jimmy informed her.

"And you have to be able to fight enemy soldiers," said Georgie.

"Yes, you have to be really brave," I added.

"Well, I can do all that," answered Rosie.

"You have to be very strong," Georgie said. "And you have to be able to climb trees really fast."

"Yeah, in the summer holidays everybody in our brigade did proper training in the woods, just like real commandos," explained Jimmy.

"Yes, and we've all won Balaclava medals," I informed her.

"That's not a problem. I could do all that," replied Rosie with supreme confidence.

Georgie and I looked at one another. I was beginning to think that we could do with another member in our brigade, but how could we be sure that she was going to be good enough. We would have to consult Colonel Michael, our leader. At that moment Michael and his younger sister, Beth, wandered down the road. Michael was a tall lean lad with large ears, which stuck out like the handles on an urn. When playing outside he always wore huge baggy short trousers, which I am convinced was a pair of his dad's long trousers with the legs chopped off. Michael's younger sister, Beth, was a delightful little eight year old with twinkling dark eyes and a beautiful fresh complexion. Her dark brown hair was always tied into two bunches with bright colourful ribbons.

"This is a new girl from Birmingham who's come to live in Stretton," said Georgie.

"Yes she wants to join our brigade," I added.

I could see from the expression on Michael's face that he was not keen to allow another girl into our company.

"I would love to have another girl in the Balaclava Brigade," Beth said eagerly.

"We've got enough people in our brigade already," muttered Michael, eyeing the new girl suspiciously.

"Well, I can do most things," Rosie said. "I won't need any special training."

Michael was not convinced.

"How do we know that you're going to be good enough?" he barked.

"We could give her some tests to do," Georgie suggested.

"That's a good idea," I agreed. "We need to make sure that she's not going to let us down when we have to face the enemy."

"I don't know what you're all worried about," said Rosie abruptly.

"I know what we'll do," said Georgie.

He turned to face Rosie.

"There's an old apple tree in our garden with a look-out post at the top. If you can climb up to that look-out post by the time Tommy counts to 20, then we'll know that you're good enough to join the Balaclava Brigade."

"O.K." said Rosie with an air of confidence. "Where's this apple tree?"

We trooped round into Georgie's garden, and stood by the wall of the old pig sty which was our brigade HQ.

"That's the apple tree and there's the look-out platform," I said, pointing up amongst the twisted branches.

Rosie stared up into the tree.

"When Tommy says *'Get ready…Get set… Go'*, you start climbing and then he'll begin counting," Georgie informed her

"O.K." answered Rosie.

I gave the order. "Get ready….Get set….*GO!*"

Upon the word 'Go' Rosie raced to the pig sty wall, leapt up onto it and started to climb. I watched in amazement as she hoisted herself onto the first bough with the utmost ease, and then clambered effortlessly upwards through the branches before swinging herself onto the look-out platform.

"I'm here," she called. "How was that?"

I had just finished counting to 10!

Beth was jumping up and down, clapping her hands enthusiastically.

"Flipping heck!" whispered Jimmy in astonishment. "Did you see that?"

There was an expression of total disbelief on Georgie's face.

"She went up that tree almost as fast as Baz can go up it," he gasped.

I was absolutely speechless. I had never seen a girl climb a tree so quickly. I watched again with total admiration as she swung down through the branches and then jumped from the pig sty wall, landing right in front of us.

"Now can I join your brigade?" she asked with a broad smile on her face.

Michael turned away disinterestedly.

I could hear footsteps running along the garden path. After a few seconds Charlie appeared, followed by his twin brother, Benny. Although they were twins, Charlie and Benny were as different as chalk and cheese. Charlie, who was always joking, was fair-haired with a round freckled face. His brother, who had a long solemn face, curly ginger hair and thick bottle-glass lenses in his glasses, was extremely clever. He had such an amazing general knowledge that we always referred to him as the Professor.

"Who's she?" inquired Charlie, rudely pointing a finger at Rosie.

"This is a new girl who's come to live in Stretton," I explained. "She comes from Birmingham, just like me. Her name's Rosie."

"Yes, Rosie's going to join our brigade," said Beth, looking around at everyone.

"Now hang on a bit, Beth," interrupted Michael. "We haven't decided yet. We don't know whether she's good enough for the Balaclava Brigade."

"But she did climb that tree really well," said Georgie.

"Yes," I added, "she shot up there much faster than most of us can climb it."

Georgie and I were both convinced that it would be a good idea to have another brigade member who was such an expert tree climber.

"We don't want any more girls in our brigade," said Charlie abruptly. "Girls aren't strong enough to be in an army brigade."

"I think I'm pretty strong," said Rosie. "My dad's a sergeant-major in the Royal Warwickshire Regiment, and when he's home on leave I usually have wrestling matches with him. I can sometimes beat him."

"Yeah and I bet he let's you win," mocked Charlie, "just 'cus you're a girl."

"Well you're not very strong, Charlie," said his twin brother, staring straight at him. "I bet you're not even as strong as she is."

"Don't be stupid!" shouted Charlie. "I'm much stronger than she is. She's only a girl!"

"OK then! We'll see which one of you is really strong," stated the Professor. "We'll do a test. Get hold of each other's right hand and then squeeze as hard as you can. Whoever makes the other one squeal first will be the winner."

"That's OK with me," said Rosie.

"And me," said Charlie, smirking confidently. "I'll take it easy 'cus you girls aren't as strong as us boys. If it starts to hurt you too much just yell 'Stop', and I'll let go straight away."

We gathered in a circle around the two combatants who were standing facing each other. As they clasped each other by the right hand we all watched intently. When Michael gave the signal for the contest to start Charlie began to exert more and more pressure, until he was squeezing with all his might. His face had turned bright red, his teeth were clenched, his knuckles were white and his hand and arm were beginning to quiver. I looked at Rosie who was standing perfectly still, her face absolutely expressionless.

Suddenly, without warning, Rosie's shoulder rose slightly and her grip tightened. Immediately Charlie let out a deafening high-pitched scream and his feet left the ground.

"Stop! Stop!" he yelled. "You're hurting me!"

Rosie loosened her grip and stepped back. Charlie held out his injured hand and stared at it. His fingers were flat and white as if a steam roller had just chugged over them.

"Look what you've done!" he screamed angrily at Rosie. "My hand's gone dead!"

"That serves you right," laughed his brother. "That'll teach you to test your strength against a *weak* girl."

"Does anyone else want to test their strength?" asked Rosie cheerily. "By the way, my right hand isn't as strong as my left one, because I'm actually left handed."

Nobody uttered a word.

"Can I join your brigade now?" she asked.

Colonel Michael could hardly refuse after what he had just witnessed.

"O.K. then! I suppose you can join our brigade," said Michael reluctantly, "but we're going to have to decide on a rank for you."

"Oh, I've already done that," replied Rosie. "I'm going to be a sergeant-major, just like my dad!"

Chapter 5

Rosie Learns about the Brigade

"We'll show you our HQ now," stated Georgie, looking at Rosie.

Our headquarters consisted of a little brick-built pig-house with a sloping slate roof, and an adjoining walled pig-pen which had been open to the sky originally. We had built a makeshift roof over the pig-pen to create an additional room. Above our HQ towered the old twisted apple tree, at the top of which we had constructed our look-out platform with a Union Jack fluttering above it. Having entered, we sat down on the very comfortable straw-filled sacks which served as seats.

"This is great!" muttered Rosie, looking around approvingly. "Now tell me all about this brigade."

"Well, we've got three different kinds of enemies," I began. "There are German spies and troops because they'll be invading our country any time now. Then there's a bully who lives in Brinton where we go to school. And there's a horrible old woman called Wilma the Witch who lives next door to us."

"And Archie Fraser's just as bad," said Jimmy.

"Who's Archie Fraser?" asked Rosie.

"He lives with Wilma the Witch because she's his grandma," I explained. "He comes from London."

"Archie Fraser should be one of our enemies 'cus he's always getting people into trouble, especially Baz," declared Jimmy.

"Yes," I said. "I think that nasty little kid is just like his grandmother – he loves being horrible to people."

"Have you seen anything of 'Mad Bull' Bullivant at Oakthorpe Senior School?" asked Georgie, looking straight at Michael.

"Who's 'Mad Bull' Bullivant?" asked Rosie.

"He's the bully who lives in Brinton," explained Jimmy. "He used to bully everybody at Brinton National School."

"I can't stand bullies," admitted Rosie. "My dad says that all bullies are spineless individuals."

"Yes," added Beth. "I think bullies are really horrible people."

"Bullivant's not in my class, but I've bumped into him in the playground quite a few times," said Michael. "He still pulls my ears when he sees me, and he always calls me "Jug Ears" and "Elephant Ears.""

"I bet he hasn't said anything about what happened at the pit head in the holidays when we were coming back from the Laurel and Hardy film?" laughed Jimmy.

"No, I bet he hasn't said anything about that!" exclaimed Georgie in a loud voice.

"What happened?" asked Rosie who clearly wanted to know everything about us.

We explained how, during the summer holidays, he and his friends had captured us at the Tunnel Top, where the main railway line goes through a long tunnel. He had pulled Beth's bunches of hair, made her cry and then shoved her so hard that she was sent sprawling onto the ground. Afterwards, when he and his mates were getting ready to take us to their den as prisoners, I saw my chance to escape so I ran away.

We also told her that a few days later, when we were taking a short cut home after our visit to the children's Saturday cinema show in the nearby town, we unexpectedly bumped into Bullivant at the pit head of the local coal mine. He grabbed hold of me and then started hitting me, so I retaliated. During the ensuing skirmish I knocked him flat on his back into a filthy ditch of coal-black mucky water. When I last saw him that afternoon he was shuffling away, his back covered in thick black mud, and he was bawling his eyes out.

"He hasn't mentioned that fight to me," Michael confirmed, "but the other day I heard him talking to one of the other kids in the playground. He said that some older mates were going to help him get his own back on that young 'Brummie' kid from

Stretton. It looks as if he's after you, Tommy. You'd better watch out!"

I was hoping that 'Mad Bull' Bullivant had learned his lesson during the holidays. But I was not so sure now! I was especially concerned to hear that he was still determined to get his revenge, and that he had enlisted the help of some older friends. I did not want to get involved in any more incidents with him. My mum had always told me that fighting was senseless because it solved nothing. When I thought about it afterwards I realised that she was right, because neither of us had actually won that fight at Stretton pit. Although Bullivant had been laid flat on his back in the mud, my bruised and grazed knuckles were sore for days, and my black eye was completely closed. The last thing I wanted was to get mixed up with 'Mad Bull' Bullivant and his mates again. Anyway, because our country was at war, there was enough fighting going on without two groups of lads from Stretton and Brinton scrapping with each other!

"What will you do if you bump into 'Mad Bull' Bullivant again?" asked Beth, an anxious expression on her face.

"I don't know," I replied. "We'll just have to wait and see what happens, but I shall try to keep out of his way."

"What are we going to do when the German soldiers attack Stretton?" asked Rosie.

"We're going to fight them!" said Michael very firmly. "Our Prime Minister, Winston Churchill, has told us that everybody must fight to defend their villages and we must *never* surrender."

"And how are you going to do that?" Rosie asked.

"I don't know," replied our colonel. "We haven't finished working out our plans yet."

"Is there anybody else in this brigade?" inquired our new recruit.

"Yes, there's Baz," replied Michael.

"Just wait till you see him!" said Georgie.

"And there's young Robbie as well," said Michael. "I don't know where he is 'cus he's usually one of the first ones here."

"P'rhaps he's got into trouble with his mum again, and she won't let him come out to play," Jimmy suggested.

Baz now burst through the doorway like a miniature charging rhinoceros. Everyone turned to look at the newcomer and Beth gave a loud gasp. We all stared at him with our mouths wide open. We could not believe what we were seeing. Baz looked totally different. What on earth had happened to him?

Chapter 6

Baz Attempts to Please

With sagging jaws and staring eyes, everyone was gawping at him in astonishment. Baz stood in front of us, his eyes flashing from one person to another.

"What's up?" he asked.

He was obviously wondering why everyone was staring at him as if he had suddenly sprouted three heads.

"What have you done, Baz?" asked Michael.

"What d' you mean?" Baz replied.

"Your hair! What have you done to your hair?" cried Georgie.

"Oh, that! Well, old 'Ardcastle said I'd got to get me 'air cut so I done it meself. I wanted to make meself look a bit better for when I 'ad to go and see 'im on Monday mornin'."

"Do you call that a haircut?" giggled Charlie. "What did you use – a blunt knife and fork?"

"No, I found these rusty old things in our shed. They was what me granddad 'ad for cuttin' the wool off sheep. I tried to cut me 'air with 'em, but I couldn't manage it very easy 'cus they dain't work very well."

"Do you mean to say you used a rusty pair of old sheep shears to cut your hair!" remarked the Professor, running his fingers through his own ginger curls. "Crikey, no wonder it looks a mess!"

Baz had attacked his abundant mop of blonde hair with disastrous consequences. Huge lumps had been hacked from his fringe so that it jagged up and down like the battlements on a castle wall, and enormous lumps had been chopped from every other part of his head. In some places his scalp was almost bald, while elsewhere huge clumps stuck out, and long straggling strands hung down like the ribbons on a village maypole.

Baz suddenly noticed Rosie sitting in our headquarters.

"What's 'er doin' 'ere?" he asked, pointing at the new girl.

"Oh! This is Rosie," said Beth. "She's come to live in Stretton, and she's joined our brigade."

"We ain't 'avin' another girl in our brigade, are we?" he cried.

Everyone was far too interested in Baz's hair to discuss Rosie's membership of the brigade.

"You can't possibly leave your hair like that, Baz," interrupted the Professor. "Poor old Mr. Hardcastle will have a heart attack if he sees you looking like that."

"Well, what can I do?"

"Yeah, what are you going to do?" asked Georgie. "You can't go to see Mr. Hardcastle on Monday morning with your hair looking like that."

"Is there anything we could rub on his head to make his hair grow again quickly?" asked Jimmy.

"There's that heap of muck in the middle of Farmer Blore's farmyard. He puts that on his fields to make the grass grow," laughed Charlie.

"I ain't 'avin' none of that stuff rubbed on me 'ead," shouted Baz angrily.

"I know!" exclaimed Beth suddenly. "Baz could wear a hat. Then nobody would see his hair until it grew again."

"It's going to take weeks and weeks for his hair to grow," I cried. "Baz can't live in a hat for the next couple of months."

Suddenly Rosie came up with the ideal solution.

"I think it's pretty obvious what we could do."

Everyone turned and looked at her.

"We could give him a proper haircut so that it looks the same all over."

I was very impressed. This girl was not only strong, agile and beautiful. She'd got brains as well.

"Eh, 'ow much 'air are you goin' to cut off," yelled Baz. "I don't want too much cut off 'cus it's getting' colder these days and me 'ead's gonna freeze."

"You're not afraid your brains are going to seize up are you, Baz?" asked Charlie. "Come to think of it that's impossible – he hasn't got any."

"That's it Rosie!" said Michael "What a brilliant idea! I'll give Baz a proper hair cut."

Immediately Baz began to look extremely uneasy.

"Now trust me, Baz, because I did a really good job when you fell into that bush in the holidays, and I had to get all those thorns out of your backside," Michael argued.

Beth was sent home to fetch a pair of her mother's scissors, and when she returned five minutes later she was clutching an enormous pair of heavy dressmaker's shears, which looked more like miniature cutters that were used for trimming the grass or the garden hedge. As Baz stared down at the murderous implement which Beth had placed on the table, his eyes widened like dinner plates.

"Eh!" exclaimed Baz, "What you goin' to do wi' them?"

The worried victim was hauled to the middle of the room where he was seated comfortably. The dirty old cloth was removed from top of the table, draped over Baz's shoulders and then tied around his neck. We gathered in a semi-circle to see how our little lance-corporal was going to fare at the hands of this inexperienced barber. Instantly Michael picked up the gigantic pair of scissors and began to cut away at the long ugly bunches of hair, and the straggling wisps which were hanging down around Baz's head. Huge matted locks and long stringy tails fell away before the shears and tumbled onto the floor. Michael worked rapidly - slashing and hacking, chopping and pruning, snipping and clipping. We watched in amazement as enormous quantities of grubby blonde hair piled up on the floor, accumulating in huge heaps like piles of dusty hay drying in the sun.

At last Michael's work was complete. The cloth which had enveloped Baz was removed, and his victim stood up. Charlie immediately exploded into a fit of giggling while Beth clasped her hand to her mouth and Rosie turned away to face the wall. The change was incredible, for the person standing before us no longer looked like Baz. The head that had once been laden with a mass of tangled blonde thatch was now completely shorn, his scalp looking more like the body of a young lamb, newly emerged from the shearing shed. His face seemed thin, pale and scrawny, and the irregular lumpy contours of his tiny skull were now all too obvious. He looked exactly like a wizened bald old man.

"It doesn't look very even, does it?" mumbled the Professor, casting a critical eye over Michael's work. "Look, there are still little bits sticking out everywhere."

"I can't help that!" protested Michael angrily, for he did not welcome that sort of criticism. "*You* ought to try cutting somebody's hair with those flipping great scissors!"

Baz clasped his hands to his head to explore the results of Michael's work.

"You've chopped all me 'air off!" he yelled. "Now look what you've done! I'm as bald as me granddad."

"It looks fine," said Michael.

"I wanna look at it! 'Ow can I see it?" cried Baz frantically. "I need to see what you've done to me!"

All the time he was rubbing his hands over his shorn scalp, endeavouring to imagine what this unfamiliar hair style might actually look like.

"It's much better than it was, but it still looks a bit messy," I whispered. "There are lots of little bits of hair sticking out all over the place."

"I think it looks much better than it did when he first came in here," argued Rosie.

Michael seemed very pleased that he was receiving a little support from our new sergeant-major.

"But how do you think we can we get rid of those little bits that are sticking out at the sides?" asked Georgie.

Michael thought for a few seconds.

"I've just had an idea," he exclaimed suddenly.

He whispered something into Georgie's ear, and my best friend lumbered off. He had been away for only a few minutes when he returned, carrying a box of matches and a packet of thin wooden spills which his dad used when lighting his cigarettes from the fire. As soon as Baz caught sight of the box of matches it brought back painful memories of that operation to remove the thorns from his bottom.

"What have you got them matches for?" he asked nervously.

"It's alright Baz, don't you worry," replied Michael calmly. "Everything will be OK, you'll see."

"You ain't going to put them matches near me 'ead, are you?" whined Baz.

"Don't worry, Baz! We'll get a bucket of water ready, just in case you suddenly catch fire," chuckled Charlie, who was rolling about on his seat.

Michael had remembered that every time he went to the barber's shop in Oakthorpe, the old chap would finish off a 'short back and sides' by running a lighted taper all round the back of his client's head to singe off any stray pieces of hair which may have been left during the cutting. When Michael struck a match and lit one of the long wooden spills it burst into flames instantly. Baz shrank down into his seat and eyed the blazing taper with suspicion. Very carefully Michael applied the lighted spill to the bits of hair which were still sticking out at the side of Baz's head. There was a crackling sound as the ends of the hairs were burnt away and a singeing scorching smell began to pervade our HQ.

"Ouch!" squealed Baz. "Watch it! You've just burnt me ear'ole!"

"Sorry Baz," mumbled Michael, his tongue waggling about between his lips, and a look of intense concentration on his face as he carefully followed the contours of Baz's bumpy skull with the flame.

Eventually Michael stood up straight. He blew out his burning taper and stepped back to admire his handy work.

"There! That looks much better now, Baz," he enthused.

"Yeah, that looks great, Baz," agreed Georgie.

"I wanna 'ave a look," cried Baz, jumping up from the seat.

Turning to his sister Michael said, "Go home and fetch a little mirror, Beth."

Beth left the headquarters and dashed off. Several minutes later I heard her dainty footsteps racing down the garden path, and she entered carrying a small hand mirror. Michael took it from her and handed it to Baz.

"There! Have a look at that! What do you reckon, Baz?"

Michael took a pace backwards, put both hands into the vast pockets of his oversized trousers, and

41

admired his workmanship with a smile of quiet satisfaction. Baz glanced into the mirror. Instantly his eyes popped out like organ stops. He could not believe what he was seeing. He dropped the mirror onto the table, and let out a deafening shriek as if he had just come face to face with a headless ghost.

"Ahgggggggg!" he hollered. "What's 'appened? What 'ave ya done? Me 'ead looks like a goosegog."

"One thing's for sure, Baz," suggested Michael, "you won't get any more nits now - they'll have nowhere to hide."

Loud peals of laughter erupted from everyone present – apart from Baz, who was looking extremely shocked and distraught.

"I ain't walkin' round Stretton lookin' like this," he groaned as he continually ran his hand over his shorn scalp.

"It looks OK, Baz. Honest!" said Georgie.

"But the cold weather's comin'," Baz insisted.

"You'll soon get used to it," I assured him. "Anyway you can always wear a hat."

"But I ain't got an 'at," replied Baz.

"Well, we'll have to find one for you," said Michael who was more than a little annoyed that Baz seemed so ungrateful.

At that precise moment, from somewhere outside, the most awful howling and wailing sound interrupted our discussion. It sounded as if someone was being subjected to a gruesome form of mediaeval torture. We rushed out of our headquarters and listened. That din was definitely coming from Brick Fields Lane beside Georgie and Jimmy's cottage. Immediately we dashed across the garden in the direction of the deafening noise. What could be happening over there?

Chapter 7

Robbie's Toy Aeroplane

Standing in the middle of the lane was little Robbie, the youngest member of our brigade, his head thrown back and his mouth open wide like the entrance to Stretton railway tunnel. We were quite used to Robbie's hollering, but this din surpassed anything that we had ever heard before. We clustered around the distressed youngster.

"What's the matter with him," said Rosie, holding her hands over both ears.

Robbie's wailing reached new heights.

"That noise is louder than the air-raid sirens at home," remarked our newest member.

"Come on Robbie, tell us what's happened," asked Beth, gently putting her arm round his shoulder.

"It's……. that…….. kid," Robbie mumbled between gigantic heaving sobs.

"Which kid, Robbie?" asked Georgie.

"That……..Archie……Fraser," came the tearful reply.

"Why, what has he done to you?" I asked.

"He.......took ......my........new.......aeroplane," sobbed Robbie, both nostrils dribbling theatrically.

Detailed cross-questioning confirmed that Archie Fraser had met Robbie in the lane when he was on his way to join us in the brigade headquarters. Robbie was carrying a new toy wooden aeroplane, which he had just received in a parcel from his dad who was away in the army. Archie Fraser had asked Robbie if he could have a look at this new toy, and once it was in his hands the mean little sneak-thief had run off with it.

"Don't worry, Rob, we'll get your plane back for you," promised Michael, "and we'll pay him back for pinching it."

"We'll definitely have to add Archie Fraser to our list of enemies now!" I exclaimed.

And so it was agreed that Archie Fraser would be included with his grandmother, Wilma Jones, as one of the enemies of the Balaclava Brigade, along with German spies and invaders and 'Mad Bull' Bullivant. But we knew that there were enormous difficulties to be overcome. When playing around the village, Archie Fraser always ran snivelling to his grandma if anybody as much as looked at him, while at school he seemed to be regarded as a clever hardworking and thoroughly trustworthy little boy, a model pupil in fact. That was the difficulty! How were we going to be able to persuade others to see Archie Fraser as he really was?

After dinner Michael, Georgie, Jimmy, Rosie and I sat on the look-out platform in the apple tree high above our headquarters, with the Union Jack fluttering proudly above us in the stiff breeze.

"How are we going to get Robbie's plane back from Archie Fraser?" asked Michael

"Go and knock on her scullery door and ask for it," suggested Rosie, as if it was the obvious thing to do.

"Well, *I'm* not going near Wilma Jones," I said. "I saw enough of her when I was living in her cottage for nearly a year."

"She's really horrible," agreed Georgie. "Nobody in our village wants anything to do with her."

"*I'll* go and knock on her door," said Rosie confidently.

We all looked at her as if she was barking mad.

"Look! There he is!" whispered Georgie, pointing through the leaves and the branches. "There's Archie Fraser, and he's playing with Robbie's aeroplane."

As we gazed down from our lofty position, we could see Archie Fraser dashing around the garden, holding Robbie's large camouflage-painted aeroplane in his right hand, and making loud roaring noises like an engine. His grandma was standing at the scullery window watching him. Hidden high among the leafy branches, we had a bird's view of the back gardens, the lane, and the rear of both cottages as well as the main road which ran in front of them.

"The little rat!" I mumbled. "He's just pinched that 'plane from Robbie and now he's running around, playing with it."

"We'll have to get it back from him somehow," muttered Michael.

Everybody agreed.

Suddenly, beyond the cottages, we caught sight of a large woman striding down the road in a very determined fashion. She was dressed in a full-length wrap-over sleeveless apron, and her hair was swathed in a blue headscarf tied in a knot at the forehead. It was Robbie's mum. Trotting closely behind was the small slight figure of a little lad, his hobnailed boots clip-clopping noisily on the pavement. Both woman and child hurried across the cottage gardens, passed beneath our look-out and headed straight for the Joneses' back door. Now we knew we were in for a little unexpected wartime entertainment! Robbie's mother was well-known in Stretton for her quick temper, while Wilma Jones was renowned for her barbed tongue and her unfriendly dealings with local people. This looked like being quite a contest!

We saw Robbie and his mum approach the back of Wilma's cottage, and then we heard a loud thumping sound, as she banged repeatedly on the scullery door. A few seconds later the door opened and Wilma stood there scowling at her unwelcome visitor.

"I've come for my lad's aeroplane," said Robbie's mum in a strong forceful tone of voice.

"Well I don't know what you've come here for," replied the old witch. "I haven't got your kid's plane."

Archie now emerged from inside the cottage to stand beside his grandmother. Robbie was hiding behind his mother's apron.

"I want my lad's plane back and I want it *now*," Robbie's mum repeated in a threatening manner.

"I don't know what you're talking about!" Wilma replied, looking down her long nose.

"A few minutes ago *he* pinched my Robbie's aeroplane," yelled the irate visitor, stabbing the air in Archie's direction with her fat finger, "and my lad only got it in a parcel from his dad this morning."

Archie shrank back.

"I haven't touched his aeroplane, grandma, honest," replied the little villain. "I didn't even know his dad had sent him an aeroplane, grandma. And that's the honest truth."

"There you are! My Archie says he didn't know your kid had got an aeroplane from his dad," repeated Wilma.

"I'm not putting up with this!" yelled Robbie's mother. "My husband's away in the army fighting for King and Country and defending us all against Adolf Hitler, and my little lad gets treated like this by an outsider, right here in his own village!"

"Well that's not true to start with," retorted Wilma, aggressively. "Your husband's not fighting Hitler's lot. Everybody in Stretton knows that he works in the army cookhouse down at Aldershot. Probably spends all his time peeling spuds and frying sausages."

"Well at least my husband's serving his country," bawled Robbie's mum, taking a step nearer to Wilma. "Soldiers have to be fed, you know. Anyway, my Jeff's not sitting on his backside all day doing nothing like your old man."

"My Cyril has served his country for years and years," insisted the old hag. "For nigh on fifty five years he slaved down that pit, lying on his back for hours on end in the cold and the damp, digging coal and breathing in all that dust. I'll have you know that men have lost their lives working down that pit. I doubt whether many army cooks have been killed by exploding sausages."

"You'd better watch your tongue," ranted Robbie's mother, who had edged forward menacingly onto the second step. "I'll have you up for slander."

The weasel-faced lad now poked his head out again.

"I can tell you exactly what happened, grandma. I saw Robbie in the lane and then I saw him drop something. When he picked it up again he started to cry. And after that he threw it over the hedge into this garden. I think he must have broken it and now he's trying to blame it on me, grandma."

"I never broke it and I never chucked it over the hedge," insisted Robbie, sniffing loudly and wiping his nose on the sleeve of his jumper.

Robbie's mum glowered down at her son, whose face now crumpled. She was obviously beginning to have doubts as to who was telling the truth.

"He grabbed it off me and ran away with it," Robbie sobbed.

"If you're telling me lies again, you know what's going to happen, don't you," his mother shouted with menace.

"I ain't tellin' lies," Robbie blurted out.

"He is, grandma. Honest he is. I'll tell you exactly what happened right from the start."

Everybody fixed their eyes on Archie Fraser, who had now adopted an extremely wide-eyed innocent sort of expression.

He continued.

"I was going down the lane and I saw Robbie with this thing in his hands. I didn't know it was an aeroplane. I said, 'What have you got there, Robbie?' He was horrible to me and he shouted, 'Mind your own business. I don't talk to smelly rats that come out of the sewers in London.' I took no notice of him because if anybody calls me names I always take no notice of them. So I started to walk away. Then I heard something fall on the ground. I looked round and he was bending over, holding that thing in his hands again. I think he'd broken it because I saw him trying to push it together, but I didn't know what it was. Then I saw him start to cry, and just after that he threw it over the hedge into the garden. That's the honest truth, grandma."

The little liar glanced first at Wilma and then at Robbie's mum to determine whether his story was having the desired effect.

"I can prove it because I can show you exactly where he threw it," he added.

Robbie was now standing behind his mum, wailing loudly with his head bowed and both his fists screwed into his eye sockets. We watched as the two women and Archie marched purposefully down the garden where they stood in a group by the hedge. Robbie trailed nervously after them, still hollering loudly.

"That's where he threw it," said Archie, pointing into the long grass by the hedge.

Robbie's mum stooped down and picked something up. The two women leaned forward to examine it, their heads almost touching.

"I told you I was telling the truth, grandma," said Archie.

"Right! That's it!" shouted Robbie's mother angrily, looking down at her blubbering son. "I'll teach you to tell lies and make a fool out of me."

She gave Robbie an almighty push in the back which propelled the poor little lad several yards forward. Immediately, Robbie exploded into an ear-splitting wail.

"Get indoors," she screamed. "Just wait 'til I get you home! I'll show this plane to your dad when he comes home on leave."

Still howling loudly enough to waken past generations from their graves in Brinton churchyard, poor Robbie turned and fled towards home like a cat with a dog snapping at its tail. His mother was striding after him in a very resolute fashion. Wilma and Archie made their way back towards their scullery door and, as they passed beneath our lookout, I noticed a mean self-approving smirk on Archie's weasel face.

"I told you I was telling the truth, grandma," he said, as they mounted the steps to go into the scullery.

We all stared at each other in total disbelief.

"I can't believe it!" I stammered. "We *actually* saw him playing with Robbie's aeroplane. It wasn't broken then."

"It was definitely Archie Fraser who broke the wing off that plane and then chucked it into the grass," stated Georgie.

"It's pretty obvious how he knew where to go when he wanted to show it to his gran and Robbie's mum," said Rosie.

"I wonder where poor Robbie is now." Georgie muttered.

I was in no doubt where Robbie had gone. When Robbie's mum was in a raging temper he always headed for the same place – the privy in their back garden. None of the houses and cottages in Stretton had an inside flushing lavatory. A Stretton toilet was a smelly brick-built hut in the back garden with a round hole cut in a wooden box, beneath which was a huge pit. Such a building was always referred to as 'the privy'.

"He'll have dashed into the privy and bolted the door," I suggested confidently, "because that's where he always hides when he's in trouble."

"Yes, and he won't come out again until he's sure his mum's calmed down," said Michael.

"Do you think we should go and tell Robbie's mum what really happened?" I asked.

"Well you can if you like!" mumbled Michael. "I'm not going anywhere near her. She still blames me for what happened when Robbie fell into that mucky cow pond, and she told our mum that it was my fault he turned up at home with no clothes on."

"He was still wearing his hobnailed boots," said Jimmy with a smile.

"I wonder how long poor Robbie will have to stay in his hiding place before it's safe for him to come out," I remarked. "He could be in there all night."

"He could be shut in there for days!" added Jimmy.

This situation was serious. Michael, Rosie, Georgie, Jimmy and I stared anxiously at each other. We would have to do something to help poor Robbie. After all, he was a private in the Balaclava

Brigade, and our motto was "All for one and one for all."

"What are we going to do?" Georgie muttered.

"We've got to do something," added Jimmy.

"Yes," I agreed, "it wasn't poor Robbie's fault, and yet he's the one who's got the blame."

"There's only one thing we can do," said Rosie.

Everyone turned to look at her.

"When one of its soldiers is in danger an army always organises a rescue."

"What do you mean - a rescue?" asked Georgie.

"We'll have to go and rescue Robbie," she said as if it was the obvious thing to do.

We stared at her. What was this girl talking about? How were going to rescue Robbie from his own privy under the nose of his own mother?

Chapter 8

Saving Private Robbie.

"My dad sometimes tells me about army rescues," explained Rosie. "If we're very careful we can get him out of that privy without his mum knowing. A proper army often has to go on special missions to rescue trapped soldiers."

Perhaps she was right. After all, Rosie ought to know. Her dad was a sergeant-major in the British army.

I could see that Rosie's idea was also beginning to appeal to Colonel Michael, too.

"I suppose we could organise an army rescue," he said thoughtfully. "But first of all we'll have to collect the other brigade members together, so that we can draw up some sort of plans."

We clambered down the tree and went in search of the others. Having assembled everyone in our brigade headquarters, we began to discuss how we were going to rescue little Robbie from his garden privy without his mother knowing. Instantly everyone sprang into army mode. This operation was going to require a considerable amount of military planning, and we knew that any rescue would have to be executed with great daring, skill and courage.

"His mum will be keeping watch on that privy door from the back of the house," suggested the Professor.

"Yeah, as soon as poor little Robbie shows his face she'll be there, waiting to grab him," said Sergeant Georgie. "And when she catches him I wouldn't like to be in his boots."

"I bet she'll have that leather strap with her," muttered Lance-Corporal Jimmy.

"Poor Robbie won't stand a chance," sighed Private Beth.

"My dad says that the army always does a recce before they begin a rescue," announced Sergeant-Major Rosie.

"What's a recce?" asked Jimmy.

"Somebody goes on a recce to spy out the land before they try to carry out their rescue mission," said Rosie. "First we need to find out if she's keeping watch on the privy door from the windows at the back of the house."

"Yeah," agreed Colonel Michael. "As soon as it's safe to begin, one of us can creep into the garden, go to the privy door, whisper Private Robbie's name and tell him to come out. As soon as he's out, the door must be closed to make it look as if he's still in there. Then Robbie can be brought back here.

Once we've got him inside our HQ, we can work out the next part of our plan."

Everyone thought that it was a wonderful idea to rescue young Robbie in this way. Very soon the Balaclava Brigade would be embarking upon one of the most daring feats in British military history. This was the brigade's big chance to cover itself in glory by saving Private Robbie. Nerves began to tingle, and everyone was quivering with excitement. Colonel Michael looked round at the assembled company, his eyes flitting from person to person.

"First we need someone to spy out Robbie's back garden so that we can decide on the best way of carrying out this operation. Captain Tommy, you're the one with the highest Balaclava Brigade medal, and so you'd better do the recce."

This order took me completely by surprise. Although I had been awarded the Order of St. George for Valour when 'Mad Bull' Bullivant had attacked me at the pit head, I had not expected to be playing such a prominent part in this vital brigade rescue operation. However, I was pleased that I had been chosen by our colonel, and I was determined that I would do my very best.

Robbie lived in the first house in the Victorian row of miner's cottages called 'Balaclava Terrace'. It was this row of houses which had provided the name for our brigade. As I walked along the main street, I paused outside Robbie's front gate. A path ran alongside the gable end of his house towards the garden and yard at the back. There was no way I was going down that path in case I accidentally bumped into Robbie's mum with that strap in her hand. There was only one thing I could do. I would have to try to observe the back of the house and its privy from the bottom of Robbie's garden. That meant running down Brook Fields Lane, climbing through the hedge and then making my way across a field to reach the end of his garden.

As I peered through the dense overgrown garden hedge, I saw Robbie's mum marching down the path towards the privy.

"Open this door!" she yelled, and she banged upon it several times.

"I ain't comin' out!" I heard young Robbie cry.

"Well the longer you stay in there the worse it'll be for you!" his mother shouted.

I heard Robbie start to wail inside his refuge, as his mum strode back up the path and disappeared. Having made a mental note of the geography of the garden and having studied all relevant information about the back of the house, I hurried back to HQ.

"She can't see the privy from any of the windows at the back of the house," I reported. "And the best way of getting there is to go down the lane into the field. But there's one big problem. The hedge at the bottom of the garden is very thick and it's got lots of brambles in it. Whoever tries to get through it will have to be very small and really quick."

"Well done, Captain," said Colonel Michael.

Once more his eyes scanned the assembled company. Eventually his gaze lingered upon one particular member. This was clearly a job for someone who was small and nimble, a person who was as fearless as lion and as quick as swiftest greyhound. There was only one person who fitted the bill.

"Right, you're the one!" said Colonel Michael, pointing at Baz. "You're our special operations expert."

The sharp-eyed, shaven-headed little lance-corporal beamed upon hearing that he had been chosen by his colonel for this very special dangerous mission. Baz was an expert at moving about unseen and unheard, and he was capable of working at the speed of lightning – unless, of course, he was supposed to be doing his school work.

"Yeah," said our lance-corporal enthusiastically. "I'm a hexpert."

"There's no time to lose," our commanding officer reminded him. "Remember all that Captain Tommy has told you. When you've rescued Private Robbie, bring him back here. And when you get back we'll take him to a safer place until his mum has calmed down. Good luck, lance-corporal!"

Lance-Corporal Baz could not wait to get on with his mission. After he had disappeared the rest of us sat around, waiting in total silence. We waited and we waited. The tension was almost unbearable. Would Lance-Corporal Baz manage to free our unfortunate private from that miserable smelly place in which he had been forced to conceal himself? Would Private Robbie's mum walk down the garden path at the wrong moment and catch both of them red-handed? This was definitely one of the most dangerous tasks our brigade had been required to carry out. The rest of us sat around in silence, waiting nervously. The minutes seemed to drag by endlessly. The silence was punctuated only by the occasional sigh or nervous cough, and the sound of people shuffling restlessly on their straw seats.

Our intrepid lance-corporal had been away for what seemed like hours when we heard the clink of metal studs on the stone path - it was Private Robbie's hobnailed boots. The bewildered private was pushed into our midst by Lance-Corporal Baz, who followed closely upon his heels.

"Well done, lance-corporal," said Colonel Michael, patting his small non-commissioned officer on the back.

We all gave a loud cheer and Baz glanced around, his face beaming. Everyone crowded around little Robbie, who did not appear to have completely come to terms with his unexpected freedom.

"We can't stay here because this is the first place she's going to look for him," declared the Professor.

"Where can we take him," asked Sergeant-Major Rosie. "I don't know Stretton very well yet."

"I think we should take him to the woods," said Sergeant Georgie.

"Yeah, we could hide him there until it's getting late, and by that time his mum won't be so angry," I said hopefully.

"I'll go and fetch the army truck," said the Colonel, "so that we can smuggle Private Robbie across the road in it."

Michael's dad, who was an engineer at the local coal pit, had made a large wooden trolley from a sturdy plank of wood, a large wooden box, two axles and four old pram wheels. It was a magnificent piece of equipment, and Colonel Michael had generously said that the brigade could use it as a multi-purpose military vehicle.

When the trolley arrived, Private Robbie was bundled into the rear compartment and covered with a piece of old black-out curtain, while Sergeant Georgie was sent aloft into the look-out post to ensure that it was safe for us to move off. From this high vantage point our sergeant gave the 'all clear' thumbs-up sign, and our company gathered around the trolley containing our hidden comrade. Slowly and carefully we moved off towards the main road like a funeral party accompanying the poor deceased to his final resting place.

As there was no traffic in sight when we reached the main road, we prepared to cross over. At that precise moment I caught sight of a large woman in a long flowery apron and blue knotted head scarf strutting purposefully along the pavement in our direction.

"Oh heck!" whispered Colonel Michael. "Robbie's mum's coming."

Chapter 9

An Unexpected Trip

"Quick!" said our colonel. "Let's get him across the road behind that lorry."

Beside the Miner's Arms on the pub square with its bonnet facing the road, was a parked lorry. It had low sides, and it was carrying a load of scrap metal concealed beneath a dark green waterproof tarpaulin.

The trolley bumped down the kerb as we hurried to get across the road. There was a loud thud from under the black-out curtain, and I heard young Robbie cry out in pain, "Ouch! My flippin' head!"

"Shut up!" whispered our colonel. "Your mum's coming."

"Quick! Get rid of him!" muttered Michael, as he pulled the trolley between the lorry and the pub wall.

Sergeant Major Rosie looked at Baz.

"Hide him!" she ordered. "And hurry up!"

It was left to Baz to conceal young Robbie while the rest of us walked round to the front of the lorry where we began to chat as if we hadn't a care in the world. Robbie's mum came striding across the road with a face like a thunderstorm.

"Where's our Robbie?" she yelled.

"I don't know," replied Michael.

"Well, when did you last see him?" she inquired angrily.

"We haven't seen him for quite a while," replied Charlie, safe in the knowledge that he was telling the truth if twenty seconds could be classed as 'quite a while'.

"He's run off, the little so-and-so," she raged. "Just wait 'til I get my hands on him."

She cast her eyes around the pub square. She stared at the lorry, and then she bent down to peer beneath it in the hope of catching sight of a pair of hobnailed boots. I was beginning to feel very nervous, and I was hoping that she did not notice our trolley. Suddenly she stopped. She had spotted the trolley with the piece of black material draped over the back of it. I held my breath as she strode towards our military vehicle, bent down and lifted the black-out curtain.

"Oh no!" I thought. " Now Robbie's going to be for it!"

She threw the black piece of cloth into the back of the trolley with a loud sigh.

"Huh!" she grunted angrily. "He's not in there."

"Phew! Well done Baz," I thought. "He's done a brilliant job this time."

Satisfied that her little son was not with us, the large lady turned and walked to the corner of the pub. There she stood for a few seconds, looking up and down the road.

At that precise moment the pub door opened and a man in blue overalls, a flat cap and huge steel-toed boots came out, smoking a cigarette. He walked into the pub square and prepared to get into the cab of the lorry. An upstairs sash window in the Miner's arms rattled up and Nora Butterworth, the pub landlady, leaned out.

"Are you ready to go now?" she asked.

"Yeah. I shan't be comin' this way for a few days, Nora," the lorry driver shouted. "I've got to take this load of stuff to Birmingham and then I've got to make some longer trips."

The man clambered into his cab and revved up the engine. Then very slowly the lorry spluttered out of the square before turning in the direction of Birmingham. As the vehicle disappeared round the corner we could hear its engine chugging noisily up the road.

Meanwhile Robbie's mother had started to walk in the opposite direction, scanning every nook and cranny in the hope of catching sight of her little lad or his hobnailed boots.

"Cor, that was a close shave!" murmured Michael.

"Yeah, I thought she was going to cop us with Robbie in the back of that trolley," giggled Georgie.

I glanced round the square. Where was Robbie? I stared down 'The Holloway' leading to Blore's Farm. Not a soul was in sight. I stared at the empty trolley. I looked at Colonel Michael and then I glanced at Sergeant–Major Rosie. They were also scanning the pub square and the lane. Every pair of eyes was darting about, searching for a glimpse of our little private.

Turning to Baz, Michael asked, "What have you done with Robbie?"

"She told me to 'ide 'im," said Baz, pointing at our new Sergeant -Major.

"I know she did but where is he?" asked our colonel.

Baz was looking decidedly uneasy.

"I shoved him in the back of that lorry!" he murmured.

We dashed to the corner and stared up the road. We could see the lorry getting further and further away from us. Then we noticed the edge of the green tarpaulin rise up to reveal a small bewildered face peering over the lorry's tailgate. We looked at one another again. There was a look of absolute horror on every face as both the lorry and Robbie's pathetic little face went further and further away from us and finally disappeared from view.

"Do you mean to tell me that you put Robbie on the back of that lorry!" cried Michael.

"Yeah," replied Baz, still staring at the ground in front of him.

"Do you realize what you've done, you idiot!" shouted Michael fiercely. "Robbie's now on his way to Birmingham mixed up with a load of scrap metal. Why didn't you say something before it drove off, you fool?"

"I couldn't say nothin', 'cus his mum was standin' on the corner. She'd 'ave found out where he was 'idin'."

"It would have been better if his mother had found out where he was hiding instead of him being carted off to some scrap metal place in Birmingham!" shrieked Michael.

"What are we going to do now?" asked Georgie, his face as white as a sheet.

What could we do? There was no doubt about it. This was the most serious situation our brigade had ever faced!

Roland Bond

Chapter 10

An Uncomfortable Night

We wandered across the road and sat on the wall outside Brown's garage. Our colonel was beside himself with anger, and he sat with his head in his hands, staring at the ground.

"Your homes are in Birmingham," said Jimmy, looking at Rosie and me. "Could one of you write to your mum and ask her to keep an eye open for him?"

"That's very clever, I don't think!" yelled Michael, without even glancing up. "A letter would take ages to get there, and by that time Robbie could have been tipped out with the scrap and melted down."

"Anyway, my mum works long hours in the factory," Rosie pointed out. "She wouldn't have time to go searching all the scrap yards looking for a little lad."

"And Birmingham is a really big place," I explained, "It's a huge city, not a tiny village like Stretton. My mum and dad wouldn't know where to start looking. There are loads of metal factories and scrap yards in Birmingham."

"What do you reckon will 'appen to 'im?" asked Baz.

"What do you *think* will happen to him?" screamed Michael. "All because of you, they'll melt him down and turn him into machine gun bullets. That's what'll happen to him!"

Everyone was devastated, and Baz was looking very shame-faced. I kept seeing that dreadful vision of Robbie's panic-stricken, little face peeping out of the back of that lorry as it trundled up the road into the unknown. Where was he now? What must he be thinking? I knew we had let Robbie down. He had trusted us and we had betrayed him. At this very moment the poor little lad was bumping along strange roads, staring out at places he'd never seen before, without the slightest idea where he was going or what was going to happen to him. Surely that was everyone's worst nightmare!

Then another terrible thought occurred to me. I knew that many of the metal factories and the scrap yards were in the industrial heart of Birmingham near to the city centre. Even if someone discovered him alive, that was the part of the city most likely to be bombed in an air-raid. It was awful to think that, while Rosie and I had been evacuated away from Birmingham to the safety of Stretton-on-the-Hill, we had just put a little lad from Stretton onto a lorry and sent him to the middle of Birmingham, where he was likely to be killed by German bombs.

Although it had been a beautiful autumn evening, I went to bed that night with my mind in turmoil. Before drawing the thick black-out curtains and getting into bed, Georgie and I stood at the window, gazing out. A full moon hung in the sky like a gigantic circular cheese, and the village street below us was bathed in a soft silver light. We stood staring in the direction of Birmingham, but on this occasion I was not thinking about my home and my parents. Tonight I was thinking about Robbie. Where was he now? What was happening to him?

When I got into bed I could not get off to sleep. But there was no noise keeping me awake. Outside there was complete silence, and Georgie and Jimmy were as quiet as church mice. As I lay in bed I kept turning over. I pulled the bedclothes over my head and then I pushed them away again. I lay on my back and I rolled over onto my stomach, but whichever position I adopted I was not comfortable. After a while I heard a click and then the door at the bottom of the stairs squeaked open. Footsteps came trudging up the stairs; every stair creaked, a doorknob rattled, the door closed and all was quiet again. Mr. and Mrs. Millward had come up to bed.

"Are you still awake, Tommy?" a muffled voice mumbled in the darkness.

It was Georgie.

"Yes. I can't get to sleep," I answered unhappily.

"No nor me," came the weary reply.

"I can't drop off, either," Jimmy called from his bed by the wall.

"I wonder where Robbie is now," muttered Georgie.

"Will he have got to Birmingham yet?" whispered Jimmy, in a manner which suggested that Robbie had gone away on his holidays. "I'm not sure how far it is to Birmingham."

"Yes. That lorry will have got there ages ago," I answered.

"What do you think will happen to him when he gets there?" asked Jimmy. "They won't melt him down with the scrap metal like Michael said, will they?"

"P'rhaps they'll find him and think he's run away from home, just like kids sometimes hide on ships to go to sea," suggested Georgie.

"Robbie might tell them that it was us that hid him on that lorry, and then we shall all be in trouble," muttered Jimmy.

"Crikey! I hadn't thought of that," I mumbled.

We all remained quiet while we thought about what might be happening to our brave little comrade. After a while Georgie broke the silence.

"Listen!" he exclaimed. "What's that noise?"

"It's your dad snoring," I replied, for Mr. Millward had just begun his nightly serenade, although the performance had not yet built up to a deafening climax.

"No, I don't mean that," Georgie insisted. "I can hear a sort of a humming sound quite a long way away."

I listened intently. Between the rise and fall of Mr. Millward's subdued grunting, I could now hear a throbbing, humming kind of sound in the distance. I very soon realised that this was the very distinctive sound of approaching German bombers.

As those planes came nearer the noise of their engines grew louder and louder, until they were roaring right over the top of our cottage. They were obviously flying extremely low because the sound was deafening. I could no longer hear the strains of Mr. Millward's rhythmical snoring, and the cottage walls were rattling and shaking as if we were in the middle of a minor earthquake. The thunderous, ear-pounding noise of those aeroplane engines seemed to be never ending. I put my hands over my ears and buried my head under the bedclothes, wondering when that terrible din was going to stop. Eventually, when all the planes had passed over, and the noise was no more than a faint droning in the distance, I emerged from my hiding place and sat up in bed.

"Georgie," I whispered.

"Yeah," came the reply.

"Those were German bombers. I've heard them before."

"They must have nearly hit our roof," Georgie answered. "I reckon there were loads of them because they were making a terrible row, and it took ages for them to go over."

"Where do you think they're going?" asked Jimmy with a hint of excitement in his voice.

"I'm not sure," I replied. "It might be Coventry."

"It might be Birmingham," said Georgie.

"Yes, it might be Birmingham," I repeated unhappily.

I had been trying very hard not to consider that possibility. I was only too well aware that my mum and dad were still living in Birmingham. Winston, my lovely old cat, was there too. He would be absolutely terrified when bombs started to explode all around. Many of my relatives and most of my friends were living in Birmingham. Rosie's mum lived there and, of course, young Robbie was there as well. I was hoping that everyone was going to be safe. From the noise of their engines and the length of time it took for those bombers to fly over, I knew that this was going to be a massive air-raid. Somebody somewhere was in for an almighty pounding.

I had glanced regularly at Georgie's dad's newspaper for any news of air-raids. I knew that the blitz had already started. Certain parts of London had taken a heavy battering, and I had looked anxiously for news of Birmingham. I was aware that at the end of August there had been raids on the Balsall Heath, Sparkhill and Small Heath areas of the city. I realised that those raids must have been the reason been why Rosie had been evacuated. Since Birmingham, like Coventry, was an industrial centre for the manufacture of aeroplanes, military vehicles, guns and shells I knew that it was an obvious target for the German air force. Now I was afraid that Robbie might find himself caught in the middle of a devastating air-raid, and I was desperately hoping that he was going to be safe. Georgie was clearly having similar thoughts.

"I hope Robbie doesn't get mixed up in that air-raid," he whispered.

"Poor little Rob!" muttered Jimmy.

"I know he's a bit of a moaner and his nose dribbles, and I know he often gets on people's nerves with his crying," I murmured, "but I wish he was back here in Stretton with us."

Georgie and Jimmy agreed, for none of us had the faintest idea what was to become of the poor little lad.

Chapter 11

Baz Drops 'a Bombshell'

I am not sure for how long we chatted or what time it was when we finally dropped off to sleep, but I was suddenly aware of Jimmy shaking me to tell me it was morning and that breakfast was ready. I looked forward eagerly to Sunday breakfast in the Millward household. Despite the rationing, every Sunday there was a rasher of bacon, some fried bread, an egg and fried potato. This was very different from the monotonous breakfasts of bread and blackberry jam which that mean old witch, Wilma Jones, had dished up for me every morning. When I was living in her cottage it was a luxury for me to have a boiled egg for breakfast, even though they kept hens and collected eggs every day.

When the brigade assembled inside our headquarters that morning, Michael, Beth, Rosie, Georgie, Jimmy, Charlie, the Professor and I could not stop talking about young Robbie.

"Where do you think he is now?" asked Jimmy.

"He's probably lying on top of a pile of scrap metal, waiting to be turned into bullets," giggled Charlie.

"It's not funny, Charlie!" shouted his twin brother angrily.

Charlie's freckled face reddened and he stared silently at the floor.

Suddenly the door was flung open and Baz burst into the room. His body was hunched up, his neck was buried beneath his shoulders and his jumper was pulled up over the top of his head. He looked like a miniature version of the Hunchback of Notre Dame.

"Blimey Baz, what's the matter with you?" laughed Charlie.

"Everybody's laughin' at me. Me mum and dad 'ave bin laughin' at me. Me gran and me granddad 'ave bin laughin' me. The woman next door 'as bin laughin' at me. I ain't walkin' round Stretton again with no 'air on me 'ead," he groaned.

"Your hair looks OK, Baz. Honest!" Georgie assured him.

"But that's the trouble! I ain't got no 'air, so it ain't OK," Baz insisted.

"Why don't you find a hat to wear then nobody will notice your hair," said Rosie.

"But I've already told you - I ain't got an 'at, 'ave I?" whined Baz.

"Alright Baz, we'll find you a hat, if that's what you want," agreed Michael wearily. "We'd all better go home and see what we can find for Baz to wear on his head."

Everyone went off in search of a hat for Baz, and we left Rosie to keep our bald little lance-corporal company. He sat unhappily in the corner, a scowl on his face and his closely-cropped cranium still hidden beneath his jumper. When everybody returned we had accumulated an impressive assortment of potential headwear.

"You could wear this," said Beth holding out her bright red knitted pom pom hat.

Baz tried it on while she held out the small hand mirror so that he could examine the effect.

"I ain't wearin' that!" he exclaimed, snatching it from his head. "That's a girl's 'at and I ain't gonna to be seen lookin' like a girl."

"What about this one?" suggested Michael, holding out a small floppy sun hat which he had worn as a young child. Michael placed it on top of Baz's head where it perched like a fairy on a Christmas tree. Baz stared into the mirror.

"This 'at don't fit me," he sulked, dragging it off the side of his head and handing it back to Michael.

"This is good one, Baz," said Georgie. "I've worn this one."

He produced the multi-coloured knitted tea cosy which he had worn when the brigade had staged its magnificent celebration parade on the pub square during the summer holidays. Georgie put it on Baz's head and pulled it well down over his ears.

"There, that'll keep your ears warm as well, Baz," he said.

"I ain't wearing this thing!" Baz yelled angrily, glancing into the mirror and snatching at the tea cosy. "It makes me 'ead look like a flippin' tea pot."

Charlie now produced a navy blue beret with a badge on the front.

"Ooh, that's a Girl Guide's badge," exclaimed Rosie eagerly. "My big sister used to be in the Girl Guides."

"Well I ain't wearin' that then!" Baz shouted instantly without even trying it on. "That's a girl's 'at and I've already told you, I ain't gonna look like a girl."

Next the Professor handed him a flat cap.

"That ain't no good!" exclaimed Baz without attempting to take it from him. "That thing's too big. It'll keep fallin' off."

"You aren't usually this fussy about what you wear, Baz," said Michael. "What's the matter with you?"

"It's this stupid 'aircut!" retorted Baz angrily. "*That's* what's the matter with me!"

Jimmy now handed him a fawn-coloured woollen balaclava helmet which his mum had knitted for him to wear during the winter. Baz dragged it over his shaven scalp, so that it completely covered his head, apart from the middle of his face. Baz stared at himself in the mirror. For the first time he looked as if he was beginning to show an interest.

"This might do," he mumbled to himself.

He studied the effect again in the mirror. He inclined his head to the left and then to the right as if he was trying on one of the latest creations in a high class fashion shop.

"Yeah. I like this 'at," he confirmed.

"Yeah, that's great, Baz," said Charlie. "It covers up all of your head – and it hides most of your face as well!"

Baz was too interested in the balaclava helmet to respond to Charlie's insult.

"That's just the job," said Rosie. "That's a balaclava helmet and you're a member of the Balaclava Brigade."

Baz gave a pleasurable little laugh, and looked at himself in the mirror once more. As he strutted around our HQ in his new helmet he was as pleased as a dog with a juicy bone.

Now that he had been given a balaclava helmet to wear Baz's needs had been satisfied, but the needs of the rest of us had not. While Baz seemed more concerned about his lack of hair and what he was going to wear to hide his lumpy scalp, our thoughts inevitably focused upon poor little Robbie.

We needed to know what had happened to him, for we were all desperately worried.

"Do you think we should go and knock on Robbie's door to ask his mum if she's found him?" said Georgie.

"No," answered Michael. "That would look as if we knew something about why he's gone missing."

"We'll, perhaps we could go and knock on the door and ask if Robbie can come out to play," I suggested. "That wouldn't look suspicious."

"Yes," agreed the Professor, "perhaps if she knows what's happened to him she'd tell us where he is."

"We already know where he is," said Charlie. "He's in Brum mixed up with a load of scrap!"

"I don't think we can go knocking on her door," said Rosie. "Just imagine that you are Robbie's mum. Your little lad has just disappeared without trace. How would *you* feel? *You'd* be worried sick! Would *you* want to be bothered by kids knocking on your door asking if he could come out to play?"

I hadn't thought about it like that! What Rosie had just said certainly put things in a different light.

After tea, when all the brigade members met up inside the headquarters, Baz was still wearing his balaclava.

"Are you still wearing that thing, Baz?" inquired Charlie.

"Yeah. I ain't gonna take this off 'til me 'air grows again," Baz replied.

"You can't wear *that* thing in school," shouted Jimmy. "Mrs. Jolly won't let you keep *that* on in class."

"And you can't go and stand outside Mr. Hardcastle's door wearing a balaclava," stressed Georgie. "He'll go mad."

"I can," replied Baz, who was waving a piece of a Wills Woodbine cigarette packet. "I've wrote 'im a letter from me gran."

"Let's have a look at it, Baz," requested the Professor, holding out his hand.

He held the fragment of card in front of his thick-lensed glasses and squinted at it.

"You can't take this to school, Baz!" he exclaimed, giggling loudly.

"Why not?" asked Baz, looking extremely puzzled.

The Professor adjusted his glasses and prepared to read the letter aloud. Everybody crowded around and peered over his shoulder. Baz's short note, written very badly in spidery pencil handwriting, read as follows:-

deer teecha

i ave rote this letta to hask if Baz cud ware is at in skool cus es got a verry bad cold in is ed and the doc sez so

Bazez gran

There were loud guffaws as everyone bent double and buried their faces in their hands. Baz looked around at us in wide-eyed bewilderment, unable to comprehend what was so funny about the literary masterpiece he had spent hours composing.

"That's one of the bestest things I've ever wrote," announced Baz.

"That's probably the only thing you've ever written," giggled Charlie.

"But Mrs. Jolly and Mr. Hardcastle will know that your gran didn't write this note, Baz," the Professor warned.

"Ooh, I 'adn't thought about that!" exclaimed Baz, clasping his hand to his mouth. "I forgot - me gran never went to school. She can't write."

"We don't mean it like that, Baz," emphasised Michael. "He'll know that you've written this letter yourself."

"Well 'ows 'e gonna know that then?" muttered Baz, looking extremely puzzled. "'E ain't 'ere, is 'e?"

"You need to get somebody else to write a proper letter for you," suggested Rosie.

"I'll write you a letter," said the Professor, "and I'll say that it's from your mum."

Baz was delighted that someone had offered to help him out of a difficult situation, because the last thing he wanted was for everybody at school to make fun of his shaven head. The Professor went off to scribe Baz's letter, and we all knew that it would be extremely well-written because the Professor was brilliant at handwriting, spelling, punctuation and grammar- in fact he was brilliant at everything in school.

When the Professor returned carrying the letter which he had written, I glanced at it. It was beautifully handwritten on a shiny piece of white pre-war writing paper and, although he was incapable of reading it, Baz was absolutely delighted.

"I'm gonna go 'ome to 'ide this letter in me room so me mum and me gran don't see it," said Baz, and he hurried away.

A few minutes later we heard footsteps racing down the path, and Baz burst back into the room at breakneck speed. He was shaking all over, his eyes were wide and bulging, and that part of his face which was visible was the colour of rolled-out floury pastry.

"What's up, Baz?" asked Georgie.

"It's Robbie!" he groaned.

"What do you mean, 'it's Robbie'?" inquired Michael.

"It were all my fault! It were me that shoved him in the back of that lorry," babbled Baz. "I were the one what done it!"

"What's happened?" asked Jimmy.

"I've killed 'im!" stammered Baz.

"Killed him!" exclaimed Michael, his mouth open and his jaw drooping. "What do you mean – 'killed him'?"

"He's dead!" Baz shrieked. "Robbie's dead!"

Chapter 12

Another Brigade Hero

There were gasps of horror from everyone and then stunned silence. We stared at Baz unable to speak or move. This was the one piece of news that nobody wanted to hear. Whatever had happened to the poor little lad? Had he tried to jump out of the moving lorry and been killed in the road? Had he accidentally been crushed when he was tipped out with the scrap metal? Perhaps he had been blown up during that massive air-raid on Birmingham. It did not really matter how it had happened. The terrible truth was that we would never see little Robbie again. Beth was sobbing quietly in the corner and the rest of us stood still like stone statues, our faces drained of colour, our eyes projecting a mixture of terror and disbelief. Somehow the members of the Balaclava Brigade would have to come to terms with the fact that poor brave little Private Robbie was dead!

Baz hurried outside and climbed up into the look-out where he sat, hunched up with his back against a huge branch.

"I can't believe it!" exclaimed Georgie, who was also close to tears.

"Robbie's been killed on active service," mumbled the Professor.

"We'll have to give him a special medal," suggested Jimmy.

"It's not much good giving him a special medal now," muttered Charlie. "He won't be around to wear it, will he?"

"They sometimes award special medals to brave soldiers after they've been killed," Rosie pointed out, for she knew about such things.

I got up from my seat, went outside, climbed the tree and sat down beside Baz.

"Baz, how do you know that Robbie's dead?" I asked gently.

There was a long pause before he answered.

"I've just seen 'is ghost," the balaclava-clad lance-corporal mumbled.

"Where did you see this ghost, Baz?"

"When I were goin' home to take me letter, Robbie's ghost went past 'is bedroom window," he explained.

"Are you sure you weren't imagining things, Baz?"

"No, I really seen it," Baz insisted. "It went across the front of 'is window and then it were gone again."

This seemed very peculiar. Baz must have been imagining things. He must have been feeling so guilty about Robbie's death that it was playing on his mind, and he had started to see strange visions. The other brigade members, who were standing in a group below us, were now staring up into the tree. I called down to them.

"Baz isn't feeling very well. He's had a funny turn and he thinks he's seen Robbie's ghost inside his bedroom window."

"I *'ave* seen 'is ghost," bawled Baz, angrily thumping the lookout platform with his clenched fist.

"He'll be better tomorrow when he's had a sleep," shouted Georgie.

"It's that haircut!" called Charlie. "It's sent him a bit funny in the head."

"I ain't funny in the 'ead!" screamed Baz, who was getting extremely agitated.

"OK Baz," I said, putting my hand on his shoulder. "We'll go along to the front of Robbie's house, and then you can show us exactly where you saw his ghost."

Pleased that I was beginning to believe him at last, Baz clambered down from the apple tree and I followed. The entire brigade trooped along the pavement behind us to the front of Robbie's house, so that Baz could show us precisely where he had seen this strange apparition. We stood in a tight group outside Robbie's front gate, staring up at his bedroom window. The empty window stared back at us.

"There's nothing there," said Michael, pointing at Robbie's bedroom window.

"I knew there wouldn't be," said Charlie laughing. "I keep telling you, there are no such things as ghosts."

"That's not what you said when we went into the haunted house in the holidays looking for that German spy," his brother reminded him.

"Poor Baz is so upset that he keeps seeing strange things that aren't really there," whispered Beth.

We turned away and began to walk back towards our HQ, leaving a confused and distressed Baz still staring vacantly at the blank window above him.

Georgie turned and called to him. "Come on Baz, there's nothing there."

Baz seemed rooted to the spot, unable to move. Suddenly he raised his arm and pointed at the front of the house.

"It's there again!" he bellowed.

Immediately everybody stopped, swung round and raced back to where Baz was standing. Baz was right! Staring up at the front of the house, I could see a vision of Robbie standing perfectly still, and he was gazing at us from his bedroom window.

"That's not a ghost," cried Rosie. "He's real!"

"You're right!" yelled Michael. "That's Robbie!"

"Look, he's got his broken aeroplane in his hand," shouted Jimmy.

"How did you get back from Birmingham?" hollered the Professor, with his hands cupped round his mouth.

Robbie shrugged his shoulders and held out his hands as if he could not hear what the Professor was saying to him.

"What happened to you yesterday, Rob?" yelled Georgie very loudly.

The response was the same. Soon Robbie's mum appeared at the window. She grabbed her son by the arm, pulled him to one side and they both disappeared.

We were delighted that we had seen Robbie, and we were extremely relieved that he was safe and well.

"But how did he manage to get back from Birmingham so quickly?" murmured Georgie.

"Yes, it was only yesterday afternoon that we saw him disappearing in the back of that lorry," remarked Michael.

"He might have come back by train," suggested Beth.

"How could he have come by train?" answered her brother sharply. "He didn't have any money."

"Do you think the lorry driver might have found him and told the police," suggested Rosie. "Perhaps they brought him home in a police car."

"Cor, I wish I could 'ave a ride in a police car," said Baz, pulling his balaclava helmet away from his lips.

"You'll probably get lots of rides in police cars before long," chuckled Charlie.

"The lorry driver might have turned his lorry round and brought Robbie straight back," suggested Beth.

"If he did, he must have come back after dark," replied Jimmy. "We were playing out 'til quite late and we didn't see him."

"I don't really care how or when he got here," I said. "Robbie's back now and that's all that matters."

Rosie changed the subject.

"Did you hear all those German bombers flying over here last night? There must have been loads of them."

"Yeah. They were flying really low," said the Professor. "I couldn't sleep so I peeped between the curtains of my bedroom window and I watched them. They were skimming the roof tops."

"I hope they weren't going to bomb the BSA factory where my mum works," sighed Rosie.

"Or the Dunlop factory where my dad works," I added.

"What's it like in an air-raid?" asked Jimmy.

"It's really terrible," replied Rosie. "When they tried to bomb the BSA factory last time, we ran to our air-raid shelter in the garden as soon as the sirens sounded. First of all, the planes dropped loads of incendiary bombs. They burn really brightly and they set things on fire so that everywhere is lit up. We could hear the ack ack guns on the ground, firing at the German bombers. Soon there was a whistling noise as the bombs started to come down, and then massive bangs when they hit the ground. Every time there was a bang I ducked my head down, closed my eyes and put my hands over my ears. Everything round about seemed to be shaking. I kept hoping that our house wasn't going to be flattened."

"I wouldn't have liked to have been there," muttered Jimmy. "I'm glad I live in Stretton."

Rosie continued.

"The next morning I went into our road collecting the bits of shrapnel from the ack-ack guns. I keep them in a box under my bed at home, and I'm going to show them to my dad when I see him next time."

I did not like all this talk of air raids. It made me feel extremely anxious.

We hung around outside Robbie's house most of the evening, but he did not appear at his bedroom window again, neither did he come out to play.

The next morning, as the bus rattled its way along the road towards Brinton National School, we all clustered round Robbie on the long back seat to listen to the amazing story he had to tell. Everyone was firing questions at him like machine gun bullets. He told us that the lorry had stopped outside a cottage on the edge of Brinton, and when the driver went into the cottage, Robbie climbed out and jumped into a ditch at the side of the road to hide.

"What happened then?" asked Jimmy.

"Well, when the lorry driver came out of the house another chap was walkin' past. They must have been friends 'cus they started havin' a chat. The bloke from the lorry said he'd got to go to Birmingham, and then to the docks."

"Crikey Rob, you could have ended up at the seaside," said Charlie laughing. "You could have taken your bucket and spade with you."

"Did you walk back from Brinton?" asked Beth.

"Yeah, I walked back through the woods."

"What time did you get back?" I inquired.

"I don't know but it was gettin' dark."

"Weren't you frightened in the woods on your own, Robbie?" asked Beth.

"Yeah. I didn't like it in the woods when it was getting dark. It was really scary."

"What did you say to your mum when you got home, Rob?" asked Jimmy.

"I said I'd run off to the woods and got lost. But I didn't get into trouble 'cus my mum was really glad to see me."

We thought that Robbie had been very courageous, and, even more important, he had not implicated any of us in his story. Everyone hailed him as an extremely brave and clever hero.

"It's all that Archie Fraser's fault," muttered Robbie. "If he hadn't broken my plane and told lies about me, I wouldn't have got into trouble with my mum."

"And if you hadn't got into trouble with your mum," I added, "we wouldn't have needed to rescue you from the privy."

"And if we hadn't rescued you, you wouldn't have ended up in the back of that lorry," said Georgie.

We were all agreed that everything that had happened was Archie Fraser's fault.

"We knew you were telling the truth about that aeroplane, Rob," I assured him. "And I can promise you that when the time comes, Archie Fraser is going to be in for quite a shock!"

"All for one and one for all," the deafening cry went up.

"Oh flippin' 'eck!" exclaimed Baz, adjusting his balaclava. "I've got to go and see old 'Ardcastle now."

"Don't worry Baz," said the Professor. "You've got my letter with you, haven't you?"

After registration Adolf, our class teacher (we had nicknamed him Adolf after Adolf Hitler), asked Georgie and me to collect all the registers from the classes and take them to Mr. Hardcastle. As we walked down the corridor, each clutching a few registers under our arms, we could see our headmaster standing outside his room with Archie Fraser on one side of him and Baz shuffling about uneasily on the other.

We paused and waited.

"For goodness sake, keep still, boy!" shouted the headmaster. "And take that silly helmet off."

"I can't, Mr. 'Ardcastle," replied Baz.

"Oh! And would you mind telling me why you are unable to take your helmet off? It is not glued to your head, is it?"

"No, Mr. 'Ardcastle."

"Well, take it off then, boy!"

"I can't, Mr. 'Ardcastle," Baz repeated.

"I will ask you once more, my lad. Why can you not take your balaclava off?"

"'Cus I've got a note, Mr. 'Ardcastle."

Baz held out the Professor's letter. Immediately the headmaster fixed his eye upon Baz's grubby little hand.

"Just look at your hands and nails, boy! They are filthy. You could grow a decent crop of potatoes under those finger nails. I know there's a war on and we're supposed to 'Dig for Victory' but that does not include your finger nails."

Mr. Hardcastle took the letter, unfolded it and his eyes raced over the contents.

"And who has written this letter, young man?"

"Me mum, Mr. 'Ardcastle," replied Baz.

"If you expect me to believe that you might as well ask me to accept that the German Kaiser won the last war."

"I dunno, Mr. 'Ardcastle, but me mum did send it," said Baz, pointing rather nervously at the letter.

"I have received many notes from your mother over the years, my boy, but I cannot possibly include this one among that number. The letters from your household are invariably scrawled on scrappy pieces of cigarette packet or some other fragment of packaging."

He glanced down at the letter again.

"What is the matter with your head, anyway?"

"Got a bad cold in it, Mr. 'Ardcastle," replied Baz, confidently. "The doc at Oakthorpe says so."

"Hmm. Got a bad cold in it," repeated the Head slowly.

"Yes, Mr. 'Ardcastle."

Baz was firmly under the impression that the headmaster had swallowed his excuse hook, line and sinker, particularly now he had mentioned the doctor.

"I see - a cold in your head and you've been to the doctor."

"Yes, Mr. 'Ardcastle."

"If that is the case, boy, why does this letter say you've got nits in your hair, and the helmet is to prevent the spread of the infection to others in the class?"

"You what, sir?" said Baz, who was taken aback by this piece of news.

"Nits, boy! You've got nits."

"I ain't got nits, sir. I've got a cold in me 'ead."

"Well why does this letter say you've got nits?"

"I dunno, Mr. 'Ardcastle, 'cus I told the Professor to write that I'd got a cold in me 'ead."

As soon as the words were out of Baz's mouth, Georgie and I realized that our young lance-corporal had made a dreadful mistake.

"Crikey!" whispered Georgie. "Baz has really put his foot in it this time!"

Chapter 13

The Look-out is Invaded

Mr. Hardcastle showed no visible reaction. He merely fixed Baz with a long cold thoughtful stare.

"Ah, so you told *the Professor* to say that you have a cold in your head - whoever *the Professor* is! Perhaps *the Professor* did not hear you correctly because he has written in this letter that you have nits."

The game was up. Baz's silence indicated that he had been forced to admit defeat.

"I shall deal with the matter of this letter later in the day," he told Baz with a sharp edge to his voice. "Now remove that helmet and give it to me. I shall not let you have it back until the end of school."

Slowly and reluctantly Baz dragged off his balaclava, revealing his bald scalp in all its glory. Archie Fraser glanced at Baz and erupted into a fit of giggling.

"Well, at least you have managed to do *something* that I have asked you to do."

"Yes, Mr. 'Ardcastle," replied Baz, shuffling about restlessly.

"That is a much more sensible hair cut — especially for somebody who seems to have a fatal attraction for head lice. It is very seldom that I am able to say with any confidence that you have been in the slightest way cooperative or obedient. Is that not so?"

"Dunno, Mr. 'Ardcastle," replied Baz.

"Now go along to class and I want both of you to report back here at playtime. You will not be going out to play this morning. I do not intend to waste any more of your valuable lesson time. Heaven knows, *you* need every bit of lesson time that we can possibly give you," he added, pointing at Baz.

Archie hurried away to join Mrs. Jolly's class and Baz slunk away behind him like a snake slithering through long grass.

Mr. Hardcastle now turned to Georgie and me.

"Ah boys! Very good! The registers! Yes, just put them on my desk, would you? Thank you, boys!"

With that he turned smartly and marched down the corridor in a soldierly fashion.

Archie Fraser appeared to have talked his way out of trouble again, for I saw him at dinnertime in the playground where he was tormenting a little girl from the lowest Junior class. I do not think Wilma came up to school to complain because Georgie and I were not summoned to go to the Head's room. As for Baz, he was made to stand outside Mr. Hardcastle's door during every bit of his free time that day. Mr. Hardcastle was clearly angry that Baz had brought a forged letter to school, but I am convinced it was only his obedience in getting his hair cut that had saved him from the worst of all punishments.

That evening Georgie and I went round to our HQ. As we glanced up into the apple tree, we could not believe what we were seeing. Standing on our look-out platform as if he owned the place was that wretched Archie Fraser. He was holding a large apple in his hand. As we stood and watched, he took an enormous bite out of it, crunching his teeth into its juicy flesh.

"Look! He's in our apple tree and he's scrumping our apples," whispered Georgie.

Suddenly Archie looked down and noticed that we were watching him. He dropped the half-eaten apple.

"What are you doing up our apple tree?" shouted Georgie.

"I'm playing," he replied.

"You're not allowed up there!" yelled Georgie.

Archie Fraser laughed.

"I'm the king of the castle and you're the dirty rascals," he chanted.

Then he started to dance about in a mocking sort of way, repeating his chant very loudly.

One by one the other brigade members arrived. Baz was quite prepared to clamber up the tree to deal with him there and then, and he would have done so had not Michael grabbed him very firmly by the jumper to restrain him.

"Get down from our tree," bawled Michael. "That's our look-out post."

"You ain't allowed up there, 'cus you ain't a member of our brigade," shouted Robbie.

"I don't want to be a member of your *stupid* brigade," the weasel-faced lad yelled back.

"It ain't a stupid brigade!" bellowed Baz, who was getting extremely angry.

He jerked away from Michael's grasp and moved towards the pigsty wall, from where he could start climbing.

"Baz!" I shouted. "Don't do it."

Peering out of her scullery window I could see the horrible face of Wilma Jones. She had obviously heard all the shouting. Suddenly she was standing in her doorway, with her hands on her hips and she was staring at us. I stepped forward and dragged Baz back from the wall.

"How are we going to get him down from our look-out?" I asked.

"I'll get 'im down if you'll let go of me!" bellowed Baz angrily.

Once again he struggled to free himself.

"We can't get him down with her watching us," said Jimmy.

"Go and tell your dad that he's pinching all your apples," suggested Rosie at the top of her voice.

"Yeah, my dad will soon get him down," Georgie shouted.

He turned and began to walk along the garden path towards his back door.

On hearing that Georgie's dad would soon be on the scene, Archie had second thoughts. He began to clamber slowly down through the foliage, his toes grubbing about for suitable footholds and his hands searching for branches to cling on to. Suddenly both Archie's feet slipped off the bough on which he was standing. His hands made a frantic grab for the branch in front of him, but his fingers were unable to cling onto it. Archie began to fall. As he bounced off the large bough below the terrified youngster let out a loud shriek. I saw him trying to grab leaves and twigs as he plummeted towards the ground at a terrifying speed.

It was very lucky for Archie Fraser that directly beneath him were Mr. Millward's gooseberry bushes, for their presence would be able to break his fall. On the other hand, gooseberry bushes are not the ideal landing-place for someone falling from a great height, since they are covered in a mass of sharp prickles. There Archie lay in the middle of the gooseberry bushes, screaming at the top of his voice.

Having watched this drama unfold from the doorway of her scullery, Wilma raced down the garden path as fast as her aged limbs would carry her. She dashed forward and dragged the howling youngster from among the spiky bushes. Squashed gooseberries and gooseberry pips decorated her grandson's hair as well as his jumper, while blood-streaked scratches covered his face, hands and legs.

As Wilma wrapped a consoling arm around Archie's shoulder and escorted him back to the cottage, the young lad blubbered, "Grandma, those horrible kids …..they were throwing stones at me……and they made me tumble out of the tree."

Chapter 14

'Mad Bull' Declares War

We saw no more of Archie Fraser that evening, and Wilma did not come round to the Millwards' house to make a complaint. Georgie's dad was in the house, and he would have been more than a match for the hatchet-faced old battleaxe. All of us in the brigade retired to our HQ where there was great rejoicing at Archie Fraser's little mishap.

"Did you see the way he hit that branch when his feet slipped off," laughed Charlie.

"And did you hear him yell when he started to fall," chuckled Jimmy.

"Best of all I liked 'ow 'e screamed when 'e 'it them goosegog bushes," admitted Baz.

"But did you hear what he said to Wilma when they went back to the cottage?" muttered Michael. "He told her that it was our fault that he fell out of that tree."

"Yes," I agreed. "We didn't throw any stones at him."

"We're not going to put up with that," declared Rosie firmly.

The next morning when Archie boarded the bus for school he looked a very sorry sight. He was covered in so many scratches that he looked as if he had been in a fight with Mrs. Clamp's bad-tempered old tom cat at the village shop. As our bus turned onto the Brinton road, Georgie pointed through the bus window.

"Look at that army truck!" he shouted.

A khaki-coloured army truck was tearing past us at tremendous speed, its headlights full on, despite the fact that it was daylight.

"That truck was full of red caps," Rosie informed everyone.

"What are red caps?" asked Jimmy.

"They're military police. They're called red caps because they have red tops to their caps," our military expert explained.

"We've seen loads of soldiers going through our village since this war started, but we haven't seen any red caps before," I muttered. "I wonder what they're doing round Stretton."

"They must be getting ready for when the Germans invade us," said the Professor.

"Yes," agreed Rosie. "I know that red caps will be making lots of preparations just before the invasion begins.

"Our dad says that Hitler's planning to invade any time now," said Georgie.

"If the Germans are coming we'll have to draw up some plans so that we can help to defend our village," said Rosie.

I was not quite sure what sort of defensive plans our brigade could come up with.

One thing was now perfectly clear. The German invasion was about to be launched. The presence of those red caps certainly suggested that the Germans would be landing in the very near future. I was absolutely certain that Rosie must be right because she knew practically everything there was to know about the army.

We saw nothing of Archie during the whole of that day. However, after school when we stepped onto the bus to go home he was already on board. He was sitting in the front seat behind the driver, who was a thin man with greying hair and a large cigarette-stained moustache. The members of the Balaclava Brigade had congregated on the long back seat as usual. Meanwhile, the driver was revving up his engine, waiting impatiently for a few remaining stragglers to arrive. As I glanced out of the window I noticed a familiar figure lumbering along the road towards us.

"Look who's coming," I whispered to the others.

"Oh heck, it's 'Mad Bull' Bullivant and he's got two big mates with him!" exclaimed Georgie. "Quick, hide behind this seat."

I slid off the upholstery and crouched down behind the back of the seat in front, so that he would not be able to see me. 'Mad Bull' ambled to the bus and hauled his considerable bulk up the steps, while his two rough-looking accomplices stood guard on the pavement. One was a tall fearsome-looking fellow with bright ginger hair and a wild look in his eyes. The other was a massive ugly-looking customer with dark hair, a swarthy complexion and a large scar running down his right cheek. They looked dirty and scruffy and they were both built like all-in wrestlers. I had never seen either of them before.

"Hey, what do you think you're doing?" shouted the driver, swivelling round in his seat to face Bullivant.

"It's none of you're business, granddad!" replied Bullivant rudely.

He turned his back on the old chap.

"Get off my bus!" ordered the driver.

'Mad Bull' Bullivant ignored him.

"I'm lookin' for that Brummie kid from Stretton," he yelled, addressing this remark to all the pupil passengers.

"Well 'e ain't 'ere," shouted Baz, from the back.

"He's ill," called out Rosie.

"He didn't come to school today," added Georgie.

I was very grateful to my friends for protecting me in this way. Then I heard a shrill voice pipe up from the front of the bus.

"He *did* come to school today! He's on the back seat and he's hiding!"

I might have guessed! It was Archie Fraser.

I could hear 'Mad Bull's' footsteps marching down the aisle of the bus towards me.

"Oy! I've told you to get off this bus," shouted the driver. "You don't go to this school anymore."

"Keep your 'air on granddad!" exclaimed the impudent bully.

"I'm going to report you," the driver threatened. What's your name?"

"Desperate Dan," Bullivant replied. "What's yours – Korky the Cat?"

"Don't you talk to me like that," the driver shouted. "Now get off my bus!"

"And who's gonna make me?" replied Bulllivant, turning round to face the furious chap.

'Mad Bull' turned to his pair of gigantic mates and grinned at them unpleasantly through the bus window.

"If you don't get off my bus I'll go and fetch the headmaster," the driver threatened.

"Well 'e can't do nothin', 'cus I don't go to 'is school no more," Bullivant replied with a toss of his head.

"Now look here! I don't have to put up with your cheek," retorted the driver. "I fought in the First War, I'll have you know. I've seen things in those trenches that would turn your stomach over. Some of my mates gave their lives for people like you, so you ought to show a little bit of respect for your elders."

Bullivant just tossed his head and laughed mockingly.

The driver climbed out of his seat, scuttled down the steps, pushed past Bullivant's huge associates and hurried into school to fetch Mr. Hardcastle. I wondered what was going to happen next. Although I could not see what was happening

I could hear everything. Was 'Mad Bull' Bullivant about to come up to the back of the bus to find me? I did not want to get involved in any more fights with him. Furthermore, I have to admit that I was pretty scared to hear that his two henchmen were a pair of gigantic muscular 'bruisers' with craggy features and fists like granite blocks.

From a few feet away I heard 'Mad Bull' Bullivant's voice once again.

"From now on it's war between me and your Stretton lot," he shouted, "Now where's that Brummie kid?"

Chapter 15

A Brigade Member Becomes Ill

Suddenly I heard Baz's voice.

"Mr. 'Ardcastle's comin'!" he shouted.

Heavy footsteps shuffled down the aisle in the opposite direction, and then a pair of heavy boots thudded noisily onto the pavement. Bullivant had jumped off the bus to join his two friends. For all his bluster and bravado, Bullivant was not intending to hang around with Mr. Hardcastle about to put in an appearance. Rosie whispered to me that my enemies had gone, so I emerged from my hiding place and peered through the back window. I could see the three of them swaggering up the road as if they owned the whole of Brinton, and they were laughing. By the time the bus driver and Mr. Hardcastle arrived, Bullivant and his two huge mates were nowhere to be seen. Our driver climbed into his seat, and Mr. Hardcastle stepped up onto the bus to stand beside him.

"Boys and girls," he began, "I wonder if anyone recognised that ill-mannered boy who was so rude to our bus driver."

"William Bullivant!" shouted all the children.

"Ah, I guessed as much," replied our head. "That does not surprise me."

Turning to the driver, he added, "He's at Oakthorpe County Senior School now. I shall have a word with the headmaster at Oakthorpe first thing tomorrow morning."

Then he turned, climbed down the steps and marched smartly across the playground.

As the bus bumped and shook its way along the road towards Stretton, there was a mixture of shock and excitement on the back seat. Everyone could not believe the insolent way in which 'Mad Bull' Bullivant had spoken to our bus driver, and there was much speculation about what would happen when the bully turned up at Oakthorpe Senior School in the morning, for the head at Oakthorpe, Mr. Grimley, had a reputation for being extremely strict. The conversation then focused on Bullivant's two ugly friends.

"Who were the two big ones with Bullivant?" asked Rosie.

I don't know," replied Georgie. "I've never seen them before."

"I don't know who they are either," said the Charlie.

"How old do you reckon they were?" asked Jimmy.

"They looked about eighteen or nineteen to me," replied the Professor.

"I didn't like the look of them one little bit," said Rosie.

"Nor me," I answered. "I hope we don't bump into them again."

I did not realise it but we were going to have quite a lot to do with those two unpleasant characters in the next couple of weeks.

"Did you hear what Bullivant said?" remarked Robbie. "He called the bus driver 'Korky the Cat'."

"He must have been reading the 'Dandy', said Jimmy.

"And Bullivant reckons that he's Desperate Dan," giggled Georgie.

"Yeah, Desperate Dan, the lavatory man," chortled Charlie.

Suddenly, with one voice, everyone on the back seat began to chant this well known verse:

> Desperate Dan,
> The lavatory man,
> Washes his face in a frying pan,
> Combs his hair
> With the leg of a chair,
> And cleans his teeth in an old tin can.

By the time we had reached the middle of Stretton all the children were yelling it over and over again at the tops of their voices. When we clambered off the bus outside the Baptist Chapel in Stretton I think the driver was very grateful that his transport duties for the day had almost ended.

"Hey, look at this," said the Professor, pointing to a poster on the chapel notice-board.

We paused to read what it said. It was an advertisement for a jumble sale at the chapel to raise funds in order to provide 'treats and comforts' to send to our brave soldiers, sailors and airmen. A jumble sale in the village was quite an event, and people would come from miles around to see what was on offer.

"I want to go to that jumble sale," said Charlie, "but the trouble is I'm broke."

"I'd like to go but I haven't got any money either," said Georgie.

It was very quickly established that everybody wanted to go, but nobody had any cash to spend.

"We'll have to find a way of earning some money," stated the Professor. "It's no good going to a jumble sale if we haven't got any money."

That evening after tea, we met in our headquarters to think up a scheme for raising money to spend at the jumble sale.

"We could do some jobs for people," suggested Beth.

"No," argued Michael, "we did jobs for people not very long ago when we needed some money to go to see that Laurel and Hardy film. People aren't going to keep giving us jobs to do."

"We could go round the houses singing," suggested young Robbie.

"What are you going to sing?" snapped Michael. "Christmas carols? Don't be daft! It's not Christmas for another three months."

"We could go round the village with the trolley selling things," suggested Jimmy.

"But we haven't *got* anything to sell," Michael replied.

We all sank back into our seats, desperately trying to think of something we could do to earn money.

"I know what we could sell!" shouted Rosie. "When I climbed your apple tree I noticed that it was loaded with big cooking apples. We could sell some of those round the village. I know that Mr. and Mrs. Fredericks in the cottage where I'm living would buy some."

"That's a great idea," agreed Georgie. "We've got stacks of apples, and there are eaters as well as cookers. I'll ask our mum and dad if we can have some. We could get quite a bit of money by selling apples."

This was a superb plan and I was so glad that Rosie had joined our brigade. But why hadn't *we* thought of that idea?

"The money we get for selling those apples should belong to the Balaclava Brigade," insisted Michael. "We're not going to use the brigade's money to buy things for ourselves."

"Well what sort of things can we buy for the brigade?" asked Georgie.

"Anything that the brigade could use to fight German soldiers," Michael answered. "Don't forget that the Germans will be landing anytime now and we've got to defend our village. We could also look for things to put in our HQ like a nice tablecloth for our table or a picture of the Battle of Balaclava to hang on the wall."

Most of us were more than happy to purchase things for the brigade, although I wondered what sort of army weapons were going to be on sale at a jumble sale organised by the Stretton Baptist Chapel. We could hardly expect it to be overflowing with implements of war like swords, daggers and bayonets!

Georgie obtained permission to pick some apples, and we gathered enough cookers and eaters to fill two large boxes which we obtained from Mrs. Clamp's village shop. However, it was soon apparent that we were facing an insurmountable problem. As fast as we picked the apples Baz kept eating them, and it was the large sour cooking apples that he liked best.

"Baz, will you stop eating all our apples!" ranted Michael. "Those apples are for us to sell, not for you to keep scoffing."

"I like these sour ones the bestest," said Baz, narrowing his eyes into slits and smacking his lips together.

"You're not having any more, Baz, or else we shan't have enough to sell," shouted Georgie. "You've eaten loads already."

Rosie informed us that her uncle kept a greengrocer's shop in Birmingham, so she offered to arrange and display the fruit to its best advantage. Using clean pieces of cloth, she supervised the polishing of the apples until their skins gleamed. Next they were carefully arranged in two cardboard boxes, one for the eaters and the other for the cookers, and finally both boxes were displayed upon Michael's trolley. I must admit that Rosie had done an excellent job, for our apples made a magnificent display.

At last we were ready to begin our rounds, so we pulled the trolley-load of apples on to the pavement and set off towards the far end of the village. We felt certain that the people of Stretton would be extremely grateful for the opportunity to buy such delicious fruit at very reasonable prices.

We had not even reached the first house when everyone stopped abruptly.

"Oh no!" yelled Rosie, putting her head in her hands.

"Blimey!" shouted Georgie, with more than a hint of annoyance in his voice.

"Flippin' heck!" exclaimed Jimmy loudly.

"You stupid little idiot!" bawled Michael, as he stared at Baz.

Everyone was glowering at our little lance-corporal.

"It weren't my fault," he mumbled, wiping his sleeve across his mouth. "I couldn't 'elp it."

"Yes you could!" bellowed Michael angrily.

Baz had been spectacularly sick. But worse than that - he had deposited the entire contents of his digestive system over both boxes of apples which we had planned to sell to the good folk of Stretton!

Chapter 16

The Jumble Sale

"What's going to happen to all this lot?" asked the Professor, pointing to our trolley- load of tainted fruit.

"Well, we can't sell them now, can we?" said Georgie.

"We'll have to throw them all away," muttered Rosie with an air of resignation.

"You've been sick all over my trolley as well," shouted Michael, staring threateningly at Baz.

"I couldn't 'elp it," Baz mumbled again.

"Yes you could!" yelled Michael. "You could have done it over there in the long grass where we couldn't see it."

"And where we couldn't smell it," added young Robbie, holding his hand over his nose and mouth.

"Anyway, you can clean it all up, Baz, 'cus I'm not touching it," bawled Michael.

"But I ain't feelin' very well," argued Baz in a pathetic voice.

"Tough!" yelled Michael. "If we start touching that stuff, we shall all be feeling sick."

"I'm not touching it," said Charlie. "You don't know what you might catch if you get *that* stuff all over your hands. I don't want to get any deadly diseases."

"What sort of diseases?" asked Robbie, looking extremely concerned.

The Professor now began to rattle off as many deadly diseases as he could bring to mind.

"Well, there's scarlet fever, diphtheria, malaria, tuberculosis, cholera, typhoid, dysentery, bubonic plague and leprosy – they're all deadly diseases," stressed the very knowledgeable Professor.

"I don't want to catch any them diseases," said Robbie very firmly with a loud snuffle, "so I ain't touchin' any of Baz's sick."

"Leprosy is the worst," the Professor informed us. "In the olden days, people with leprosy had to warn other people that they were coming. They had to go around shouting *Unclean! Unclean*!"

"I reckon we should get Baz to walk round Stretton shouting *that* all the time," laughed Charlie. " 'cus he's never clean."

"What are we going to do with all these apples?" Rosie asked. "We can't just dump them here by the side of the road, can we?"

"We could wash 'em and then we could still sell 'em," said Baz helpfully. "Nobody'll know what's 'appened."

"Ugggh, we can't sell *those* apples to people now," said Beth, wrinkling up her nose.

"No, we can't let people eat *those* apples after what you've done to them," said Rosie firmly.

"We don't want the people in our village gettin' leprosy or that plague," remarked Robbie. "It might spread and then I might catch it."

Georgie, Michael and I agreed that we could not possibly sell contaminated fruit to the villagers of Stretton.

"Can I 'ave them apples, then?" asked Baz, his eyes lighting up. "I can wash 'em and take 'em 'ome to me mum."

"I don't care what you do with them as long as you get rid of them from here," snapped Michael.

"You could wash them in the stream down by the bridge, Baz," said the Professor.

"And while you're there," added Michael, "you can wash my trolley. That's an order!"

"But how are we going to get some money for the jumble sale?" asked Rosie.

"Yes," agreed Beth, "I was looking forward to going there."

"Do you think your mum would let us pick some more apples," I inquired.

"Yeah, I should think so," answered Georgie. "I'll ask her 'cus we've got tons of apples."

Therefore it was agreed that, while Baz went to the stream to wash his apples and clean Michael's trolley, Georgie would ask his mum if we could pick some more apples. Having obtained permission, we climbed the apple trees to gather a fresh supply of eaters and cookers to sell. The twins went to the village shop to ask for two clean boxes in which to display the fruit, while Michael accompanied Baz to the stream to superintend the cleansing of his trolley, before taking it home to rinse it down with some of his mum's extra strong disinfectant. He was not taking any chances that a few deadly germs might still be lurking on it.

As soon as Michael came back with his clean trolley, everyone started sniffing noisily.

"Pooh that trolley stinks worse than it did after Baz had been sick over it," stated Jimmy, turning his back on it.

"Cor, it's horrible," added Robbie, holding his nose.

"What have you put on it?" asked Georgie, pulling a face.

"Our mum's disinfectant," replied Michael. "It's really good strong stuff."

Rosie was pointing at the trolley.

"We can't put these new apples in that trolley now," she argued. "It will make them smell of disinfectant and then nobody will want to buy them."

"We'll just have to take it in turns to carry the boxes then," I suggested.

Michael and I each picked up a box, and we set off on our rounds for the second time.

At the first house we approached we stopped abruptly beside the garden gate. A gigantic dog, tethered to a long metal chain, was guarding the path, growling and snarling at us. Its huge eyes stared as if it considered us to be its next meal; its tall pointed ears were erect, and its enormous jaws, like a massive medieval man trap, were slightly apart to reveal a set of ferocious white fangs.

"I'm not opening that gate with a German Shepherd Dog there," said the Professor.

Baz looked at the dog and then at the Professor.

"Is that a Jerry sheepdog?" he inquired.

"No it's an Alsatian," said Michael.

"They're the same thing," replied the all-knowing Professor. "Some people call them Alsatians; other people call them German Shepherd Dogs."

"If that's a Jerry sheepdog, then it's got to be one of 'itler's dogs," announced Baz.

"Here we go again!" I mumbled to myself.

Baz gawped at the ferocious animal which glared back at him with eyes that seemed to be daring him to set foot inside the gate. I thought for one split second that Baz was preparing to enter into mortal combat with this Nazi creature. After all, once before he had inflicted a crushing defeat upon a young Friesian bull because he was convinced that it was a Nazi, having been informed that Hitler had conquered Holland, the country from which this particular breed of cattle originated.

Baz continued to stand by the garden gate, staring into the dog's eyes as it crept forward slowly, its top lip curled, its teeth bared, and low deep growls rumbling in the back of its throat. Suddenly the fierce beast lunged forward, barking and snarling, its heavy chain rattling and jangling. When the massive hound hit the gate feet first, we all jumped back and dashed away in fear of our lives.

"They ain't gonna get none of our apples," proclaimed Baz triumphantly, "'cus they've got one of 'itlers dogs at that 'ouse."

Having made this important announcement, Baz was obviously under the impression that he had achieved a decisive victory. He clearly thought by that denying this household the opportunity of purchasing some of our delicious fruit he would be striking a fatal blow against the entire German war effort.

From that point onwards our apple-selling expedition was a tremendous success. Without exception, our customers remarked how beautiful our apples looked, and we could have sold more if we had been able to carry them. When we returned to our headquarters we counted out the money to discover that we had raised the princely sum of 4 shillings and 6 pence, which was not an insignificant amount for us. Michael argued that the money ought to be divided according to rank, the largest sum going to the Colonel of the Brigade and the smallest amounts being allocated to the two Privates. The rest of us insisted that it should be divided equally.

"All for one and one for all!" we cried.

"If we all have the same amount how much will I get?" asked Jimmy.

While the rest of us were trying to work that sum out by counting on our fingers or scribbling away in the dirt with bits of stick, the Professor had already arrived at the answer.

"Everybody will have sixpence," he said nonchalantly.

The Professor was brilliant at arithmetic, and I could never understand how he worked things out so quickly.

When the Friday evening of the jumble sale arrived the members of the Balaclava Brigade, each clutching six pennies, were at the front of the queue, waiting for the doors to open. We were determined that we were going to have the pick of the items on sale. Soon more and more people arrived until there was a long queue which snaked around the building, through the gates and along the village pavement.

Eventually the doors were thrust open and we dashed into the hall. Rushing across to the large 'white elephant' and toy stall, we descended upon it like a plague of hungry locusts attacking a field of ripened corn. I cast my eyes rapidly over the items on display. A long series of trestle tables were covered with a multitude of articles of all shapes and sizes. There was so much to look at.

Before I had chance to closely examine any of the items on view, I heard a loud voice which caused me to turn around. I peered through the throng of jostling people, and my heart sank! On the other side of the room was 'Mad Bull' Bullivant. Even more worrying was the fact that he had brought his frightening friends, Scarface, and Ginger along with him. Who were those two hideous creatures? Why had they suddenly arrived in Brinton? And what were *they* doing at our village jumble sale?

Chapter 17

A Narrow Escape

I was fairly sure that they had not seen me yet. Although I had been looking forward to this jumble sale for almost a week, I knew I could not stay in the chapel hall with those three thugs wandering about. Ringing in my ears were the words uttered by Bullivant on the bus, "Where's that Brummie kid?" I knew that I would have to escape and hide somewhere until they had gone back to Brinton. Quickly I started to push my way through the heaving crowd of people towards the exit. Once outside I could race into Georgie's garden and hide inside our brigade HQ.

Suddenly a voice boomed out.

"There 'e is!"

I glanced over my shoulder. 'Mad Bull' Bullivant's finger was pointing directly at me, and his two ugly accomplices were staring menacingly in my direction. I had been spotted!

Desperate to get away as quickly as possible, I pushed my way towards the exit, dashed out of the hall, ran down the path and into the street.

Along the village pavement I fled. On reaching the Jones's front gate, I unfastened the latch and charged through the gateway, slamming the gate shut behind me. I raced round to the back of the Jones's cottage and sprinted down the garden path. I could see that the Jones's privy door was standing slightly ajar as usual. This privy was somewhere where I could hide in safety! On many occasions in the past, when I had been living with the Joneses, that little brick-built privy had been my place of refuge. Once inside, I could slide across the huge iron bolt which secured the door, and I knew that this smelly little out-building would be the ideal place to save me from Bullivant and his mates.

I barged open the solid wooden door and dashed inside. Suddenly I stopped dead in my tracks. My body froze and my eyes opened wide! I could not believe what I was seeing! There before me, in royal splendour, sat Wilma Jones like a majestic queen upon her pine-box throne, her feet slightly apart, her ample skirts now rumpled up around her waist and a gigantic pair of shiny blue drawers enveloping her knees and legs. For a split second I just stood absolutely still, staring at her. Her panic-stricken eyes were staring back at me. Her look of absolute shock and horror must have matched the expression on my face.

Suddenly she let out a prolonged high-pitched squeal, and snatched at her enormous under-garment. What was I to do now? At that precise moment I was not sure which was the lesser of two evils – to stand there staring at Wilma whilst she sat in state, or to escape outside and run the risk of bumping into a rampaging 'Mad Bull' Bullivant accompanied by Scarface and Ginger. In an instant I had made my choice. Without uttering a word, I turned tail and fled, leaving the privy door wide open and Wilma in full view.

I heard the front gate slam shut as the trio came charging into the garden. They were still coming after me. Where could I hide? I thought about making for our headquarters, but for some reason which I am unable to explain, I clambered up onto the pigsty wall and climbed into the old apple tree. There I crouched upon our look-out platform, totally hidden from view but able to peer out between the leaves, the branches and the large cooking apples. I saw my three pursuers run round the corner of Wilma's cottage into the back garden where they began a frantic search. Now they were directly beneath me.

"He must be 'ere somewhere," shouted the ugly brute with ginger hair.

"We'll soon find 'im then," cried his massive friend with the jagged scar running down his cheek.

I saw the three of them creeping towards our headquarters. I watched with dismay as they disappeared inside. I was extremely concerned to think that Bullivant had discovered our brigade HQ, but I was feeling pretty relieved that I had chosen to hide in the apple tree. It was several minutes before the three thugs emerged again.

"Well 'e ain't in there," muttered the ginger-headed one.

"He must be 'idin' inside that place!" muttered 'Mad Bull', pointing towards the Jones's privy door, which was now closed again.

I watched as they tiptoed across the garden and stood in front of the solid privy door. Ginger pushed gently against it. When it refused to open they were clearly convinced that I was hiding inside. Immediately the three of them began hammering on its wooden boards and kicking them.

"Come on! We know you're in there!" bawled Scarface.

"If you don't come out we'll bust the door down and come and get you," yelled the ginger-haired one.

There now arose from inside that privy a deafening shrill scream, like that of an off-key operatic soprano endeavouring to reach that unobtainable high note. Instantly 'Mad Bull' Bullivant and his two cronies leapt back from the door and looked at one another, totally perplexed. Obviously they had been startled by that unnerving high-pitched shriek. Spinning round, they dashed up the garden path and disappeared round the corner of Wilma's cottage. I heard the front gate slam as they fled, and from my hiding place high in our brigade look-out I could see them dashing up the road in the direction Brinton, fleeing like terrified rabbits scurrying back to the safety of their burrows.

Several minutes later the privy door was flung wide open and Wilma emerged, still clutching her long crumpled skirts around her waist, but her shiny outsized underwear now hoisted back into position. She glanced anxiously around the garden and then raced up the garden path, screaming "Cyril! Cyril!" As she mounted the steps and disappeared into the scullery, I smiled inwardly, for I was quietly pleased. Two of the brigade's bitter enemies, Wilma the Witch and 'Mad Bull' Bullivant, had just given each other the fright of their lives.

Believing that it was safe for me to emerge from my hiding place, I climbed down from the apple tree and ran to our brigade headquarters. When I opened the gate and peeped inside I saw a scene of total devastation. Our seats and our table had been overturned; the tool chest with the hinged lid, which served as our cupboard, had been hurled over onto its side; and our rag rug had been ripped up from the floor and thrown into a corner. Our brigade headquarters was a total wreck!

Chapter 18

A Multitude of Purchases

I knew that our Colonel was not going to stand for such a blatant attack on our HQ. But how were we going to stop 'Mad Bull' Bullivant, and his two cronies, both of whom were built like heavyweight boxing champions? I did not dare return to the jumble sale in case Bullivant and his pals had gone back inside. Instead I tidied up the headquarters, putting each piece of furniture back into position.

I was relaxing on one of the seats, wondering how I was going to avoid bumping into 'Mad Bull' Bullivant in the future, when the other members of the brigade came through the doorway carrying an assortment of purchases.

"Where's Michael?" I asked.

"When I last saw him he was trying to get some money knocked off the price of something he wanted to buy," said Rosie.

We heard Michael's footsteps, and he struggled into the pig sty, laden with goods like Father

Christmas doing his rounds on Christmas Eve. He placed them on the floor and sat down.

"What did you get Tommy?" he asked with a hint of excitement in his voice.

"I couldn't get anything," I replied, "because when 'Mad Bull' and his mates came into the jumble sale they spotted me and I had to run away. Then they started to chase after me."

"What happened?" asked Georgie.

"I rushed out of the chapel hall and ran into Wilma's garden. Then I decided to hide in her privy. When I shoved open the door and went inside I nearly died because Wilma was there, sitting on the toilet."

Everybody roared with laughter.

"What happened then?" asked Georgie, chuckling away to himself.

"She squealed out loud," I replied with a giggle, "so I rushed out again and climbed up to the look-out post."

"Where were Bullivant and his friends?" asked Beth nervously.

"They were hunting around in the garden, looking for me," I answered. "The problem is they've discovered our HQ because I saw them go inside. They tipped everything over and made a real mess, but I've tidied everything up again."

Everyone in the brigade was furious that 'Mad Bull' Bullivant, Scarface and Ginger had been into our brigade headquarters and trashed it.

"We can't let them get away with that!" exclaimed Michael indignantly.

"Yeah, but what can we do about it?" muttered the Professor.

"I'm not getting mixed up with Bullivant any more," I said.

"Nor me," agreed Georgie.

"We'll have to find a way of dealing with 'Mad Bull' Bullivant and his mates," stated our leader, "so we're going to have to think up some very clever plans."

After a few seconds spent deep in thought, Michael continued excitedly. "What's everybody bought then? First of all, I'll show you what I've got."

He bent down and picked up an old farmyard pitchfork, which had once been used for moving hay and straw, although one of its pair of long curving prongs had been snapped off.

"This was a great buy!" exclaimed Michael. "I got this for a penny."

"What use is that?" asked Baz. "It's busted."

"This, my little friend, is a first class weapon for capturing German soldiers when they invade us," said Michael. "This long handle with one sharp spike on the end will be much better than a soldier's bayonet."

Michael certainly had an eye for a useful piece of equipment, and a bargain.

"I've also got this silver-coloured cup," he said.

"What's that thing for then?" Charlie inquired.

"This," announced Michael proudly, "is the Balaclava Cup. It's our brigade's most valuable treasure, which we will keep safely in our headquarters."

"That's a great idea," said the Professor, "because all army regiments have regimental silver."

"That's right," agreed Rosie. "Regimental silver is always very valuable, and they keep it locked away very safely."

"Finally I've got this," stated Michael, holding up a large framed needlework picture, containing the flags of the First World War Allies and the names of some of their important battles. Embroidered in the centre was an army field gun.

"I'd only got two pence left," he continued, "and she said this picture was three pence. But in the end she let me have it for two."

"Well what use is that," said Charlie dismissively. "Unless you're thinking of smashing it over the head of a few German soldiers."

"This wonderful picture, "explained Michael, "will be hung on the wall of our headquarters. Every time we look at it, it will remind us that we are fighting for something very important, just like the chap who did this picture."

"The soldier who made that picture must have been in the Royal Artillery," said Rosie.

"Yes! That's definitely the badge of the Royal Artillery," agreed the Professor, pointing to the embroidered field gun on wheels.

I thought that Michael had spent his money very wisely.

"What have you got Georgie?" asked our leader, who obviously could not wait to see what the others had bought.

"I've bought this old horn," our sergeant replied, holding up a long brass and copper hunting horn. It makes a really loud noise."

He lifted it to his lips and blew into it, causing such a deafening blast that everyone clamped their hands over their ears.

Michael seemed quite pleased.

"Yeah! That's quite good. It makes a noise just like an army bugle, only much louder. "

"We could blow that thing when we go to fight them Jerries," said Baz.

"And I've bought this golf club," added Georgie. "This wooden bit on the end is really hard and it will make a smashing weapon if we come across any German soldiers."

Michael stretched out his hand and felt the hard wooden end of the club.

"Yes. That will be a great weapon for capturing Germans," he agreed.

Next Georgie stooped and picked up an enormous black iron poker with a huge round knob on one end.

"It's a bit bent," said Robbie in a whinging tone. "Anyway, that ain't no good 'cus we can't have any fires in our headquarters. We ain't got a fireplace or a chimney"

"I didn't buy it to poke fires," explained Georgie. "This will make a super weapon, and we'll keep it inside our headquarters in case a German spy comes creeping round here."

"That's a good idea," said Michael, " 'cus our dad keeps a wooden pickaxe handle behind our back door in case a German spy comes near our house."

"And I've got this fancy table cloth as well," Georgie said.

He produced a bottle-green chenille table cover with tassels all round the edge. Unfortunately there were several large singe and burn marks in the middle of it.

"It's a bit damaged," said Charlie, looking down his nose at it.

"Well, she let me have it for a penny," replied Georgie. "I think that was cheap."

"You've done pretty well, Georgie," said our leader. "What did you buy Jimmy?"

Jimmy held up a large chipped and cracked Victorian vase with one handle missing.

"I've got this vase for our headquarters," he replied.

Michael stared at Jimmy. He did not appear to be very impressed.

"What the heck did you buy that thing for?" he shouted.

"It'll look lovely on the top of that cupboard," Jimmy explained tentatively.

"Is that the only thing you've bought?" asked our leader with an edge to his voice.

"I got these as well," replied Jimmy uneasily.

From the floor he picked up a large rusty axe and a garden spade with the top of the handle missing.

"What the devil have you bought those things for?" bawled Michael. "We've already got a chopper and a shovel. We found them here in the pigsty when we cleaned it out."

Jimmy looked extremely disappointed that his purchases did not meet with our leader's approval.

"I've got this," said the Professor, holding up a woodworm-infested wooden rattle. "Farmers used to have bird-scarers like this one to scare birds from their corn fields."

"What makes you think we need a bird-scarer?" cried our colonel. "We haven't got any corn fields and we don't need to scare birds. It's German soldiers that we need to scare, and I don't think they're going to be frightened by the sound of *that* thing!"

"I've got this book as well," the Professor mumbled anxiously.

He held up an ancient battered and torn copy of 'The Essential Family Doctor'. He began to flick through its tattered pages, and as he did so Baz glanced at it.

"That ain't no good!" Baz blurted out. "That ain't got any pictures in it. I can only read pictures."

"Why the devil have you bought *that* book?" shouted Michael.

"If anybody in our brigade becomes ill we can look in here to see what's wrong with them," explained the Professor.

"That's a good idea," said Charlie, laughing. "Now we shall be able to see if anybody's caught one of those deadly diseases from Baz."

From the expression on Michael's face he was not thrilled with the items chosen by the Professor.

"What did you buy Charlie?" inquired our leader.

Charlie held up a novelty salt and pepper cruet set. The salt pot was in the shape of Stan Laurel and the pepper pot was modelled on Oliver Hardy.

"What have you bought salt and pepper pots for?" yelled Michael, who was becoming more than a little hot under the collar.

"Well, everybody likes Laurel and Hardy, and I thought it would look nice in our headquarters."

Michael shook his head in disbelief.

"I've got somethin' really hextra special," said Baz, who could hardly wait to show us his purchase.

He held up a dome-shaped brown and black bakelite radio set with no plug on the end of the flex.

"That's really good, ain't it?" enthused Baz with a toothy grin. "We can sit in our 'eadquarters now and 'ear on the news if them Jerries is comin' to attack us. Then we can be ready for 'em!"

"That's no good, Baz!" exclaimed young Robbie. "It ain't got a plug on it."

"We could get a plug to put on it," suggested Jimmy.

"It's rubbish!" shouted Michael. "It's a load of old rubbish."

"Why's that?" inquired Baz, looking very surprised. "I thought it would be good for findin' out about them Jerries."

"We can't plug it in!" Michael bawled. "That's why! There isn't any electricity in a pigsty, you little idiot. Just in case you didn't know, pigs don't spend their spare time listening to the wireless!"

Baz looked extremely crest-fallen.

"Well, I've got these little plates and this table cloth as well," said Baz, holding up four small cracked tea plates, and a gigantic badly-stained white tablecloth with several large holes in it.

Michael sighed deeply and sank back into his seat.

"We're not planning on arranging a tea party for Hitler's lot when they come, you know!" he bellowed angrily.

"But you said we needed a tablecloth for our table," insisted Baz.

"That thing's too big and it's ten times worse than the one we've already got," shouted Michael. "I meant a nice tablecloth – one that's in good condition."

"Look what I've bought," cried Beth, holding up a straw hat, the brim of which looked as though it had been nibbled by an army of hungry mice. "I can wear this when we have our next parade."

She also held up a brass table gong attached to two polished cow horns mounted on a shiny wooden stand. Accompanying it was a beater on the end of which was a leather-covered ball.

"And what use are those things going be to an army of fighting men, Beth?" said Michael curtly.

"I think they look really nice," she replied, as she lowered them down onto the floor again.

"I bought this," said Robbie, holding up a small brass bell which made a gentle tinkling sound as he shook it. "I thought we could use it to warn everybody when the Germans are coming."

"Warn everybody!" bellowed Michael. "Do you think that thing is going to warn everybody? I can hardly hear it and I'm sitting next to it. I don't know what use you think that's going to be as a warning. It's not exactly the bells in Brinton church tower, is it?"

"What else have you got there, Robbie?" asked Georgie

"I've bought these Dandy and Beano comics as well," he answered proudly. "I thought we needed things in our headquarters to read. But *this* is the thing I like the best."

He held up a white shiny oblong Victorian plaque with pink colouring around the edge.

"I think this pink colour looks lovely," Robbie enthused. "I thought it would look nice hangin' on this wall."

We all stared at the object as Robbie held it aloft. Our eyes were drawn to the words printed in the centre of the plaque - 'Prepare To Meet Thy God'.

"That's flippin' great, I don't think!" screamed Michael. "Just imagine that the German soldiers are attacking us. We glance up at the wall. All we can see is 'Prepare To Meet Thy God'. How do you think that's going to make us all feel? Do you think that's going to cheer everybody up?"

Michael put his head in his hands and muttered under his breath. I could quite understand why Michael was not thrilled. After all, a plaque containing the words 'Prepare To Meet Thy God' would certainly not boost the spirits of a brigade facing the enemy.

"I've bought these," said Rosie, picking up a silver-coloured metal whistle and a small battered leather case, from which she took an ancient pair of black binoculars. "I thought the whistle would come in handy if we needed to call for help," she said. She put it to her lips and gave a deafening blast on it.

"And these glasses will be really handy for keeping watch on enemy troops."

"These are really brilliant," exclaimed Michael, examining the field glasses.

He paused for a few seconds.

"I knew we should have dished out most of the money to the colonel, the captain, the sergeant-major and the sergeant. We're the only ones who've bought things that are any good. The rest of you have spent your money on a load of old junk."

He cast his eyes around at the items which some people had bought.

"There's a radio we can't use, some stuff we've already got, a warning bell you can't hear, several things that might be OK if we were holding a party for Hitler's army and a plaque that tells us we're all going to die. I just don't know what we're going to do with all this useless rubbish."

"We could stick it in another jumble sale," chuckled Charlie.

Michael looked thoroughly fed up.

"Some of you lot need to start bucking your ideas up," our leader warned. "The Balaclava Brigade's in trouble. We've got Archie Fraser, who keeps getting on everybody's nerves. Even worse, 'Mad Bull' Bullivant's discovered our HQ and now he's declared war on us. We've also got to be watching out for German spies and soldiers. The trouble is that Archie Fraser's got Wilma Jones to protect him; those two ugly blokes are always with Bullivant; and we've got no idea when the Germans are coming."

Michael was right. The Balaclava Brigade had a great deal to worry about!

Roland Bond

Chapter 19

The Handkerchief Inspection

"Go on Baz," shouted Georgie.

"Well done!" yelled the Professor.

We were playing a game of football in the playground before the start of school. The Stretton kids were playing some of the Oakthorpe kids. Two sets of gas masks placed against the churchyard wall served as one set of goal posts, while another goal was similarly positioned at the opposite end of the playground against the wall of the school air-raid shelter. Baz and Rosie, our two forwards, were the star performers in our team. Baz was agile and quick, and he had a surprisingly good shot for a little lad. What is more, he could dribble the ball just like Stanley Matthews, that amazing wizard of the dribble who played on the right wing for England. Rosie was also fast, very strong in the tackle and she had a shot like the cannon on a Crusader tank.

I always played just behind Baz and Rosie in the middle of the pitch, while Georgie and Charlie were both experts in defence. Beth normally went in goal since she tended to keep picking the ball up whatever position she played in. The Professor and Robbie usually wandered around aimlessly, occasionally kicking the ball whenever it happened to come their way. The problem was that Robbie's aim was not very good. However, it has to be admitted that his contribution could be quite useful, for on more than one occasion he had a saved us from almost certain defeat. Many times in the past, when he had lashed out with his hobnailed boot, he had missed the ball completely and delivered a full-blooded blow on an opponent's shin or ankle. It was not unusual for Robbie's lethal hobnailed boot to have reduced the opposition to half strength by the time the school bell rang.

Our team members were now shouting encouragement to Baz because, having received an inch-perfect pass from Rosie, he was dribbling his way up the pitch as if the ball was attached to his toe on a piece of elastic.

"Hit it Baz!" shouted the Professor, who had temporarily left the pitch for a rest. He was now sitting down reading a Dandy comic, his back resting against the air-raid shelter wall.

"Shoot Baz," yelled Robbie as he bent down to tie up the lace on one of his lethal hobnailed boots.

The score was 5 goals each and time was running out. Soon Adolf, our teacher, would be appearing at the door to ring the hand bell for the start of school. Baz was now within range of the goal and was shaping up to score.

"Shoot!" shouted Rosie.

"Go on!" yelled Charlie, who was running up from behind. "Hit it, Baz!"

Baz steadied himself, looked up at the goal and let fly with a terrific shot. It zoomed past their tiny goalkeeper who, on seeing the ball flying towards him like an anti-tank shell, decided to take refuge behind one of his very large defenders. When the ball crashed against the wall between the gas mask boxes a huge cheer went up from everyone in the Stretton team. Baz had scored another fantastic goal which was surely going to win the game for us.

Unfortunately that was not all that he had done! At the very moment Baz hit the ball, his right boot parted company with his foot. It looped high into the air and cartwheeled over the wall into the churchyard next door. But on this occasion the result was particularly dramatic.

Several of us ran towards the churchyard wall to see if we could see where Baz's boot had landed. As we approached the edge of the playground, a large pair of hands clasped the coping stones on top of the wall. Next there appeared a black hat which was perched at a drunken angle upon a mass of untidy white hair. Very slowly a fat red face came into view, a small pair of glasses sitting drunkenly across a broad nose and a shiny lump rapidly developing on one side of this chap's forehead.

I very quickly realised that this person peering over the wall was the vicar of Brinton, the Reverend Digby-Smythe. With a puzzled expression on his face, he straightened his glasses with his podgy fingers. Next, his eyes darted around the playground in the hope of discovering who had dispatched that flying boot at his head. He must have had a very good idea, for Baz was hopping around on one booted foot, the other one raised off the ground clad only in a wrinkled sock which displayed a hole so large that all five of his grubby little toes were clearly visible. Our vicar said nothing, but vanished again behind the wall as quickly and as mysteriously as he had appeared.

Adolf, our teacher, now appeared at the school door, and the hand bell rang out loudly across the playground. All the children stood perfectly still, and upon hearing the bell for a second time, everybody assembled quickly and silently into class lines to be marched to their classrooms with military precision – everybody that is apart from Baz, who had limped off in the opposite direction to retrieve his boot from among the ancient gravestones.

Today was the one day in the month when the Vicar of Brinton came to conduct a service of morning worship, and to talk to the whole school.

After registration, the classes trooped into the hall one by one to be seated on the floor in their rows. Whilst he was waiting for the vicar to arrive, Mr. Hardcastle decided to carry out his weekly handkerchief inspection. Soon the probing cross-questioning began.

"Right, girls and boys! Who has not brought a handkerchief with them this morning? Take them out and hold them up in front of your faces where I can see them."

There was much shuffling and fidgeting. Soon a host of hankies and bits of rag of assorted shades of grey were fluttering and waving about like the sails on Nelson's fleet at the Battle of Trafalgar.

"Boy!" shouted Mr. Hardcastle. "When did you last have your handkerchief washed?"

He was pointing vaguely into the middle of the hall towards a lad whose hanky looked like a cross between a dirty dish cloth and an oily rag.

"Not sure, sir," replied the lad.

"It looks as if that handkerchief has never been washed since the war started."

"Yes, sir," agreed the boy.

"And you boy, where's your handkerchief?"

"I dropped it on the floor this morning, and the dog ripped it up, sir."

"I trust that it was cleaner than the disgusting nose wipe that we have just been looking at," said Mr. Hardcastle.

"And where's yours," he asked in a loud voice, pointing at Robbie.

"I ain't got an hanky," replied Robbie, sniffing loudly.

"Do you mean to say that you do not possess a handkerchief?" asked the Head.

"Yes, sir," Robbie answered honestly.

"Well, if you do not possess a handkerchief, how can you possibly blow and wipe your nose?"

Baz now piped up.

"'E blows and wipes it on 'is jumper, Mr. 'Ardcastle," Baz shouted out.

To draw attention to himself in this way was most unwise of Baz, for Mr. Hardcastle's eye was now riveted upon our bald-headed lance-corporal. Normally Baz ducked down out of sight behind the person in front when there was to be a handkerchief inspection, for like Robbie he never carried a hanky.

"And where is your handkerchief, may I ask?"

"I've lost it, Mr. 'Ardcastle," replied Baz.

"And where exactly did you lose it?"

"In the snow, Mr. 'Ardcastle," came the reply.

"You lost your handkerchief in the snow!" shouted the Head. "We haven't had snow since last February and it is now October. I suppose you also wipe your nose on your jumper?"

"Yes, Mr. 'Ardcastle," replied Baz.

There was a brief pause, before Baz spoke up again.

"But my nose don't dribble like 'is does," he added as an after thought, as if to soften the impact of his first response.

"All those children without handkerchiefs will report to my room at the beginning of playtime. Do you understand?"

The entire school chorused, "Yes, Mr. Hardcastle."

We now had to endure a lengthy and wearisome lecture about nasal hygiene. Mr. Hardcastle spoke at great length about the value of handkerchiefs in dealing properly with coughs and sneezes.

"Coughs and sneezes spread diseases," he reminded us. "If we are going to defeat Hitler we all need to keep fit and free from infection. To have clean noses will enable us all to remain healthy and it will help us to win this war."

I glanced around the hall. I could not help feeling that our headmaster was wasting his time, since little Robbie was sniffing loudly and swiping the back of his hand under both nostrils, while Baz was extremely busy pushing his right index finger as far as he could up his left nostril.

When the vicar arrived to take assembly the Head stood aside. The Reverend Digby-Smythe was dressed in a black suit with a gleaming white dog collar and silver cross around his neck. He was a short rotund man with red cheeks, a shock of bushy white hair, a pair of small wire-framed spectacles perched on the end of a bulbous nose and a large swelling positioned above his left eye. The vicar beamed at his assembled congregation, for he seemed delighted once again to have the opportunity to give his talk to the young children before him. Little did the reverend gentleman know what problems awaited him.

Chapter 20

The Vicar Takes Morning Worship

"Good morning, children," the vicar began.

"Good morning, vicar," crooned the assembled school, as if it were the first line of Bing Crosby's latest popular song.

"We shall begin our little service this morning by singing *'All things bright and beautiful',*" he announced.

As Mrs. Jolly thumped out the first few bars on the piano, I glanced around at the bleary-eyed muddle-headed array of children around me, and I could not help thinking that our vicar could have chosen something far more appropriate to commence our morning worship.

When the murderous rendition of that hymn had been completed, the vicar began to tell us a Bible story about the army of the Jews facing a horde of Philistines across the battlefield. He told us how the gigantic Philistine leader, Goliath, dressed in a helmet and armour made of chain mail and carrying a huge seven foot sword, had paraded in front of the Jewish army, taunting and challenging them. The reverend gentleman went on to inform us that Saul, the leader of the Jews, did not take up Goliath's challenge.

"Does anyone know why Saul did not come out to fight Goliath?" the vicar asked.

One hand shot up. A boy was kneeling up, his arm waving about furiously, and he was shouting at the top of his voice, "Sir! Sir! Sir!"

It was Baz.

I had noticed that Baz had been listening very intently for once. It must have been talk of armies, armour, helmets and fighting that had attracted his attention. Since Baz was obviously the only child who knew the answer, the vicar pointed at him.

"I am very pleased to see that somebody knows their Bible stories," said the smiling vicar.

Baz could scarcely wait to provide the answer.

"Yes, why did Saul not come out to fight?" the vicar asked once more.

'Cus he were a yeller belly," answered Baz.

The vicar was rather taken aback by this response.

"No, it was not because Saul was afraid," he said politely. "It was because he was not feeling very well."

"Yeah, but yeller bellies always say that when they're scared," called out Baz, who clearly had very firm views about such matters.

Mrs. Jolly was bending forward from the piano stool, desperately trying to attract Baz's attention so that further embarrassment could be avoided, but Baz was not looking in her direction.

The vicar then told us how David, a young poorly-clad Jewish shepherd boy, stepped forward to fight the giant Philistine.

"Does anybody know how David defended himself against that formidable opponent?" the vicar asked.

For the second time one hand shot up. Once again it was Baz. Immediately Mrs. Jolly turned away and buried her face in her hands. Since nobody else's hand was raised the vicar pointed at Baz once more.

"Yes. How would he have protected himself?"

"With a tin 'at and some 'and grenades," Baz shouted out.

There were muffled sniggers from among the children, and all the teachers turned to face the wall.

"No," said the vicar, displaying great patience. "No, he did not have access to a steel helmet or hand grenades. He was armed only with a home-made sling, some small pebbles and, most important of all, he had *God* on his side."

"Did 'e have a tin 'at and some 'and grenades, then?" yelled out Baz.

The vicar paused, took a deep breath and chose to ignore that remark altogether.

Baz sat enthralled as the vicar went on to narrate how young David had swung the sling above his head several times before releasing his stone, which struck the giant on the forehead, causing him to stumble and fall.

"And what do you think happened after that?" asked Reverend Digby-Smythe.

Once again Baz was convinced that he knew the answer. Without waiting to be asked he shouted out.

"They give 'im the Victoria Cross!"

"No. They did not have Victoria Crosses in those days," explained the vicar. "Having felled Goliath, David leapt forward, grabbed the giant's huge sword and chopped off his massive head."

On hearing this thrilling piece of news Baz completely forgot himself. He leapt to his feet, threw his arms in the air and cheered at the top of his voice as if a goal had been scored by his favourite forward playing for Oakthorpe Rovers. Everybody looked round at him. Mrs. Jolly could remain seated no longer. She stood up, waded in amongst the mass of children's legs, grabbed hold of Baz by the arm, and hauled him to the end of the row to sit down beside her

"Now girls and boys, what lesson do you think we can learn from this wonderful story," asked the vicar.

Immediately Baz's hand shot up again, but this time Mrs. Jolly was ready. She bent forward, grabbed hold of Baz's arm and pushed it firmly by his side.

The vicar concluded by saying that it was not always the biggest and the strongest who win the battle. He went on to point out that Hitler's army was bigger and more powerful than ours, and yet everyone in our country knew that we were going to defeat Hitler's evil regime because our country was in the right and we had God on our side. I knew that the members of our brigade had never been in any doubt that we would beat Hitler, but the vicar's words gave me some hope that we could find a way of defending ourselves against 'Mad Bull' Bullivant and his two colossal companions. David versus Goliath seemed instantly to take on a different meaning.

During afternoon playtime I was talking to Georgie, Jimmy and the twins when weasel-faced Archie Fraser came across and stood with our group. We stopped talking and looked at him.

"My dad's stronger than your dad," he said, pointing at Jimmy.

"No he isn't," responded Jimmy, "'cus my dad's really strong."

"But my dad's got really big muscles, because he lifts lots of heavy things at work," continued the weasel-faced little creature.

"But my dad's got massive muscles, 'cus he works down the pit digging coal," replied Jimmy.

"Well my dad used to live in the toughest part of Glasgow," Archie boasted.

"Well my dad used to be a heavyweight boxer," shouted Jimmy, leaning forward and staring into his opponent's face.

"My dad could batter your dad any day," replied the little trouble-maker.

"Does your dad work in a fish and chip shop, then," giggled Charlie.

Archie looked annoyed.

"No!" he yelled. "My dad works at the London docks."

Baz now came over and joined the group. Immediately Archie turned his attention to our shaven-headed comrade.

"My dad's stronger than your dad," Archie began again, prodding a finger towards Baz.

"No he ain't," shouted Baz. "'cus my dad's really strong."

"But my dad could beat your dad with one hand tied behind his back," the little trouble-maker said with a sneer.

Baz was beginning to lose his temper. I saw his muscles tense and his fists clench.

"Don't Baz," I said. "He's not worth it. He's trying to get you into trouble."

"Your dad's a weakling! Your dad's a weakling!" Archie chanted, as he jumped up and down and then backed away to a safer distance.

"Baz darted forward and made a lunge at Archie, who jumped back even further and ran away to stand beside Mrs. Jolly.

"Please Miss. Those boys are trying to get me," the little sneak moaned.

"We're not, Miss," said Jimmy. "He keeps causing trouble."

"Now stop it, all of you," called Mrs Jolly. "Leave each other alone. We don't want any squabbling or fighting in this playground."

"The sneaky little so and so!" murmured Georgie.

"He does that all the time," said Jimmy. "He does it in class. He starts trouble and then he goes to the teacher and says it's our fault."

"I ain't 'avin' 'im sayin' my dad's a weaklin'," said Baz

Archie had certainly found Baz's vulnerable spot.

"Fighting him isn't the answer," I told Baz. "I know he's made you mad, but hitting him won't do any good. He wants you to hit him so that he can get you into trouble."

"Tommy's right," said Georgie.

Georgie turned his face aside and muttered, "Somehow we've got to find a good way of stopping Archie Fraser, that's for sure."

"Yes," I agreed, "but I don't know how we're going to do it!"

Chapter 21

Operation Goliath.

We were sitting inside our brigade HQ.

"This headquarters looks really great now," observed Georgie, glancing around.

I looked at our recent purchases. All the weapons had been placed inside the pig-house for safety. The green chenille tablecloth had been draped over the table in the centre of the room, its fringe of tassels hanging down. On top of it Beth had carefully placed her decorative dinner gong and her straw boater to cover up the singe and burn marks. The framed embroidered picture, the hunting horn and Robbie's religious plaque had been hung on the wall. The Balaclava Cup, Jimmy's Victorian vase and Charlie's Laurel and Hardy cruet set were decorating the top of the cupboard, while Robbie's pile of comics and the Doctor's Book lay casually upon one of the seats as if someone had just finished reading them. Rosie's whistle had been safely placed inside the cupboard, alongside her binoculars.

"We're not standing for 'Mad Bull' Bullivant and his mates raiding our headquarters," stated our colonel.

"What are we going to do then?" asked Robbie.

"I think we should do the same to them," suggested Rosie. "We should raid their HQ."

"That is exactly what we are going to do," said Michael.

He stopped and considered for a few seconds before continuing.

"But we're going to do more than just raid it. We're going to wreck it! We're going to completely destroy it! First of all we'll have to draw up our plans very carefully without anyone knowing. This is going to be a really important top secret military operation and we need a code name for it."

"We could call it 'Operation Goliath' after the story the vicar told us in assembly," suggested Rosie. "Real soldiers use names like that for their special operations."

"Yeah, that would be great!" shouted Baz, who was still highly excited about the brave young shepherd lad who had killed the Philistine giant in battle and chopped off his head.

"I think that would be a really good code name," I said, "because we're up against a stronger enemy just like David was."

Everyone thought that 'Operation Goliath' sounded very army-like, but we knew that detailed plans for this important and daring mission would have to be very carefully prepared. Our colonel began his detailed briefing, explaining precisely what preparations we needed to make, what we must take with us and how we would go about carrying out our mission. We were warned that we must talk to no one about these plans; nobody must have the slightest suspicion that one of the boldest and most courageous raids in military history was about to be undertaken.

"You know those notices that have been stuck up in town," said Michael. "You know – the ones that say 'Careless Talk Costs Lives'. Well, remember! You never know who might be listening so everyone must be very careful. 'Operation Goliath' is top secret."

Suddenly Charlie pointed towards Baz.

"What's that you've got sticking out of your pocket, Baz?" he asked.

"It's me catapult," replied our lance-corporal, pulling the weapon out and holding it aloft. "I've made it meself."

Baz's new weapon had been constructed from a forked piece of a branch and a length of rubber inner tube from inside a bicycle tyre.

"I'm takin' this into battle with me," he continued. "If I get near 'Mad Bull' Bullivant I'm gonna shoot him."

He pulled from his other pocket several round stones.

"Don't be so stupid, Baz," said Georgie. "You could knock his eye out with one of them."

"You could even kill him," said Jimmy.

"You're not shooting that thing at anybody," insisted Michael. "If you do some serious damage to Bullivant with that you'll have PC Poynter coming to your house."

Baz seemed bitterly disappointed that he was not allowed to take his newly made catapult into action.

At school, during the rest of that week, a little group of children could be seen huddled in a corner of the playground, conversing in silent whispers, their heads close together. During the evenings we would gather inside our headquarters to engage in similar secret consultations. When the important Saturday morning of the raid arrived the sun was shining. As we hurried across Farmer Blore's field, our nerves were tingling and our limbs were quivering with excitement and anticipation. Corporal Charlie was holding the rusty chopper in one hand while Lance-corporal Jimmy was carrying the large axe over his shoulder. There was much chopping and hacking to be done. This time the brigade meant business, and Bullivant's camp, where he hatched his evil plans, was going to be completely wiped out.

"Brigade! Halt!" yelled our Colonel as we reached the edge of the wood.

Everybody came to an abrupt standstill.

"Right now, chaps, remember the plan," Colonel Michael whispered. "We have gone over it loads of times, so we should be able to carry it out with our eyes shut."

We climbed the stile and set off along the woodland path. Somehow this did not seem to be the right sort of day for carrying out an act of wanton destruction. Beams of mellow autumn sunlight pencilled through the canopy of foliage above, casting flickering pools of light upon the woodland floor. Birds fluttered and chirruped in the tree tops, and the woods were rich with the fruits of nature - large clusters of vivid red rowan berries, small blackish-blue plums dotted among the blackthorn trees, and bunches of deep purple elder berries which glistened as the sunlight caught them.

As we approached the Brinton side of the woods, our Colonel signalled for the brigade to stop.

"There it is in that ditch at the edge of the field," he whispered. "Now that we can see their den we'll take cover behind these bushes."

He paused for a few seconds.

"Right, we need somebody to take a look a closer at the den to make sure that it's safe to move forward," he announced.

"I'll go!" said Lance-Corporal Baz. "I'm a hexpert."

"No, I'll do it," whispered Sergeant-Major Rosie.

She was already creeping forward, and our bald-headed lance-corporal was definitely not pleased that he had been overruled. I watched as Sergeant-Major Rosie crawled and slithered through the long grass and the bracken. She moved in a huge arc, skirting the open clearing which lay between us and Bullivant's den. The rest of us lay hidden, watching and waiting anxiously. Eventually, our sergeant-major returned.

"I managed to get right up to it," she whispered. "But we've got a problem. There's somebody inside it. I could hear them talking and laughing, but they didn't see or hear me."

"I reckon it's the same three who were there when we found this den in the school holidays," murmured Colonel Michael.

On that occasion we had seen 'Mad Bull' Bullivant and two smaller lads visit the hide-out.

"How are we going to wreck their den with them inside it?" muttered Sergeant Georgie.

"We'll have to find a way of getting them out of there," whispered the Professor.

Suddenly Lance-Corporal Baz jumped to his feet and dashed into the middle of the clearing, where he stood facing the den. His chest was puffed out and there was a defiant look upon his face. Then fumbling inside the front of his jumper he pulled something out. It was his home-made catapult. Next he began to pace slowly up and down the clearing, his deadly catapult at the ready, his eyes fixed on the den.

"What's the stupid little idiot doing?" muttered our Colonel. "This wasn't part of our plan."

"And look! He's brought that catapult with him!" whispered Sergeant-Major Rosie.

Chapter 22

The Brigade's Plans are Ruined

Now Lance-Corporal Baz was standing facing Camp Bullivant, his feet apart and his catapult at the ready. Suddenly he delved his hand into his trouser pocket and pulled out a stone. Next he loaded his catapult, and held it in front of his chest.

"You're all yeller bellies!" our lance-corporal bawled loudly.

"He's gone stark raving mad," murmured Colonel Michael. "He's off his flipping rocker."

"Come on out! You're a yeller belly, Bullivant!" bellowed the intrepid little fellow, raising his loaded catapult in front of his face.

We peered anxiously towards the entrance to the den, but nothing seemed to be happening.

"What does the silly little fool think he's playing at?" mumbled Colonel Michael.

Baz's voice rang out once more.

"Come out and fight, you big fat weaklin'," he screamed.

"Baz, come back!" called Private Beth in a loud whisper, but he could not hear her.

"I ain't scared of you, Bullivant, and I ain't scared of your mates," taunted the little fellow.

"He's not right in the head," mumbled the Professor.

"Have you only just discovered that?" muttered Corporal Charlie.

"I reckon he thinks he's David getting ready to fight Goliath," I whispered.

"All this is the vicar's fault," complained Lance-Corporal Jimmy. "He shouldn't have told us that story at school."

"Perhaps we shouldn't have called this mission 'Operation Goliath'," whispered Sergeant-Major Rosie.

"Come on, you big fat ape! Are you scared to come out?" our lance-corporal bellowed.

"I'll kill him when I get my hands on him," murmured our Colonel between clenched teeth.

"I reckon you might be too late," mumbled Corporal Charlie, "Bullivant will probably beat you to it."

Suddenly there was a movement at the entrance to the den. All eyes were fixed upon it, and then a figure started to clamber out of the ditch. It was 'Mad Bull' Bullivant.

"Oh heck, he's coming out," mumbled Robbie. "Baz has had it now!"

Bullivant lumbered into the grassy clearing and swaggered confidently in the direction of his victim, a furious expression on his flabby face. He was a large hulk of a lad with long dangling arms and oversized hands. Our brave lance-corporal stood his ground, his trusty catapult ready for action.

"Don't come no closer, gorilla face!" Lance-Corporal Baz warned, and he spat the words out.

It was quite obvious that Bullivant was not going to be deterred by Baz's warning. In fact, the little fellow's insults seemed to be spurring 'Mad Bull' on, for the bully looked angrier than ever. He continued to shuffle forward, his hanging cheeks crimson, his eyes blazing and his mouth snarling like that of a tormented guard dog.. Now he was within range of the little lance-corporal.

Baz gave one final warning. "Stop there, you big fat yeller belly!"

Bullivant took no notice. Still he lumbered on towards Baz. Without further warning our lance-corporal drew back the rubber of his catapult as far as it would go, took careful aim and released his deadly missile.

At any moment I expected to see the large bully collapse on to the ground in a heap, howling with pain as the stone hit him. Instead he was still shambling forward. I could not believe what happened next. I watched in amazement as the stone from Baz's catapult looped gracefully into the air in a gentle arc and plopped down harmlessly about a yard from where our lance-corporal was standing. As the stone bounced on the ground in front of him, Baz peered down at it with large round staring eyes. He was totally perplexed.

Then I noticed another movement at the entrance to the den. This time two larger figures clambered out of the ditch. It was Scarface and the ginger-headed brute. Now they were striding across the clearing towards Baz.

"Oh crikey! Those two twerps were in there with him," murmured our colonel. "Quick chaps, let's get going! It's every man for himself!"

I was already on my way, for I did not need a second invitation to get away from that place. We all started to crawl and slither away as fast as we could through the long grass and tall bracken. But I was very anxious about Baz. Why was he still remaining there, with Bullivant, Scarface and Ginger bearing down on him?

Chapter 23

The Balaclava Cup

As I crawled away I paused and stretched up to have one last glance over my shoulder into the clearing. I could see that Baz was still standing his ground, facing the oncoming trio. Surely he was not going to stay there! Everyone knew that Baz was a little thickhead, but I did not think that even he was stupid enough to remain behind to face those three vicious brutes! Realising that there was nothing I could do to help him, I scurried away through the undergrowth.

As soon as I thought it was safe to do so, I stopped crawling, jumped to my feet and started to run. I was still a long way from Stretton, for Camp Bullivant was on far side of the woods, close to Brinton village. I sprinted as fast as I could, and I continued running until I had left Bullivant's den far behind. After a while I slackened my pace, because I was gasping for breath and my legs were aching.

As I bent forward with my hands on my knees, I heard a voice calling my name.

"Tommy! Tommy!"

I stopped and looked around, but I could see nobody.

"Tommy! It's me. I'm over here."

That voice seemed to be coming from behind a clump of bushes on the other side of a wide ditch. I jumped across the ditch, crept cautiously towards the bushes and peered behind them. There lying on the ground, clutching her right ankle was Sergeant-Major Rosie.

"I could see you through these bushes, Tommy, but I'm afraid I hurt my ankle when I jumped across that ditch," Rosie groaned. "I can't walk on it, Tommy. Can you give me a hand, please?"

"Rosie!" I called, "Don't try to move until I've had a look at it."

Her ankle was already quite badly swollen.

"You can't walk all the way back to Stretton on that ankle," I said.

"Well, I'm not lying here behind these bushes all day," she replied. "Come here and give me a hand."

I bent forward and hauled her into an upright position until she was standing on one leg.

"Now put your arm around my shoulders," I said, "and I'll support you."

She did as I instructed and I slid her arm around her waist.

"You'll have to keep your swollen foot off the ground as much as possible," I warned.

As we struggled slowly through the woods I was reminded of a picture I had once seen in Cyril Jones's newspaper. It was a photograph of two soldiers fleeing from the German army as they tried to reach the Dunkirk beaches, so that they could be rescued. One of them was wounded and his comrade was almost carrying him.

"We're just like a real pair of British soldiers now," I thought.

It seemed to take ages for us to hobble through the woods and across Blore's Field. When we finally reached the pub square we crossed over the road and headed for our headquarters so that Rosie's injured ankle could be treated.

The others were already there, but the Professor had only just arrived before we did.

"This idiot got lost 'cus he took the wrong path," chuckled Charlie, pointing at his brother.

The Professor looked at his twin over the top of his thick-lensed spectacles as if he could have strangled him.

"How did you manage to get lost in Stretton Woods?" asked Jimmy. "We've been through there loads of times"

"I got in a bit of a panic and I didn't see the right path," admitted the embarrassed Professor, adjusting his glasses with one finger.

"You should eat more carrots," said Jimmy, "'cus they make you see much better."

"Yeah. That's true," confirmed Georgie. "We saw this big poster a few weeks ago and it said you should eat plenty of carrots 'cus they're good for your eyes, especially in the blackout."

"How do they know carrots are good for your eyes," inquired young Robbie.

"That's obvious, stupid," giggled Charlie. "You never see horses, donkeys and rabbits wearing glasses, do you?"

He roared with laughter.

We examined Rosie's swollen ankle while the Professor consulted his doctor's book to see how we should treat it.

"It'll be alright when I've rested it for a bit," said Rosie.

"This book says that you should put something really cold on it," said the Professor. Therefore we decided to take Rosie to Georgie's wash house where she could put her foot under the cold water tap. Michael offered to fetch the Balaclava military vehicle to save her walking, but she declined the offer. Convinced that there might still be some of Baz's deadly germs lurking on it, she informed him that she would rather hobble round to the wash house like a real wounded soldier.

As she stood with her injured foot resting in the large brown sink, the icy cold water splashed all over her ankle. Suddenly she looked sideways at me.

"Thanks, Tommy," she said. "I don't think I would have made it back here without you."

I was delighted that I had been able to help her in her hour of need.

"Well, our brigade motto is 'All for one and one for all'," I reminded her. "I think any of us would have done what I did."

"Hey, what's happened to Baz?" asked Georgie, for he had noticed that everybody had returned to base apart from our lance-corporal.

"Do you think Bullivant's lot have captured him?" said the Professor.

"Well if they have, it's his own stupid fault," snapped Michael in a manner which suggested that he could not have cared less.

"I hope those three haven't got hold of him," muttered Jimmy.

"Well, he was asking for trouble when he was shouting those names at them, wasn't he?" said the Professor.

We waited in our HQ until it was quite late but Baz did not turn up. What on earth could have happened to him?

Chapter 24

Baz Turns Up

The following morning the members of our brigade met up on the corner of the street outside the Miner's Arms. It was Sunday morning. Rosie said her foot now felt much better although I noticed that she still walking with a limp.

"Has anybody seen Baz this morning?" inquired the Professor.

"No," replied Georgie, "I hope he's alright."

"Baz is a really fast runner," observed Jimmy. "I don't think those three would be able to catch him."

"Don't worry!" chuckled Charlie. "Baz is just like a monkey. If he had to, he would get away by swinging through the trees."

"I'm a bit worried about him," said Georgie. "Baz is usually out playing by now."

Although the rest of us were anxious about our little lance-corporal, Michael seemed totally disinterested. It was obvious that he was still extremely annoyed that Baz had totally ruined our carefully planned raid on Bullivant's camp.

I glanced up the road. Shuffling along the pavement was a bent old lady with wispy white hair, nostrils like rabbit holes and a wrinkled leathery face which had collapsed in the middle like a punctured football. She was wearing an ancient pair of tattered slippers, thick stockings which were crumpled like corrugated cardboard and a large pinafore apron decorated with a multitude of stains of every size and colour. It was Baz's gran.

"'Ave you seen our Barry?" she asked, sucking on her gums.

"Blimey, she hasn't seen him either," mumbled the Professor.

"No," I replied. "We haven't seen him since yesterday."

" 'E's been and pinched me false teeth," she moaned. "I can't eat nothin' without me false teeth."

She sucked noisily on her naked gums again.

"When did he do that?" inquired Charlie, turning away from her and trying desperately hard not to laugh.

"This mornin' before breakfast," she spluttered, spraying everybody with tiny droplets from her mouth. "I 'aven't 'ad no breakfast yet because of 'im. I'll give 'im such a beltin' when I get 'old of 'im."

She sucked her toothless gums again, wiped her hand across her crinkled lips, turned awkwardly and shuffled away to search for Baz and her false teeth.

"Well that means he must be safe then," the Professor said. "If Baz pinched her false teeth this morning, he must have come home last night."

That certainly seemed very logical. We did not call him the Professor for nothing!

"But why didn't Baz let us know he'd come back?" asked Georgie.

"Yeah, he should have come to tell us that he was back," said Rosie. "We could have sent out a search party to look for him just like they do in the British army."

"P'rhaps his mum and dad or his gran wouldn't let him go out again last night." suggested Michael.

"That's never stopped him before," chuckled Charlie.

I glanced up the road again. Baz's gran had disappeared, but now I could see a small hunched figure creeping along the pavement, occasionally dodging into a gateway or behind a hedge whenever he saw somebody. There was no mistaking who it was. It was Baz. His blonde hair, which had now started to grow again, stuck out at right angles all over his scalp like the tiny bristles on a bottle brush. As he came nearer I noticed a large bluish-purple bruise to one side of his face, and grazes to both his knees. He seemed to holding his left arm carefully across his chest as if he was in pain.

"Are you alright Baz?" I asked, as we clustered around him. "What happened in the woods yesterday?"

"Me catapult dain't work, and me stone shot up in the air and nearly 'it me on the 'ead."

"But what happened next?" asked the Professor.

"What do you think 'appened?" replied Baz. "I chucked me catapult at 'em and run like mad."

"But how did you hurt your head and your knees and your arm, then?" inquired Rosie.

"Oh that!" giggled Baz, as if it was nothing. "Well, I went in our 'ouse 'cus I needed a drink of water 'cus I'd bin running fast. Then me gran said I couldn't go out no more. I told 'er I'd got to go and see me mates, but she said it could wait 'til mornin'."

"But Baz, how did you get hurt," yelled Georgie impatiently.

"Well, I told 'er I'd got to go, so I started runnin' away. When I were nippin' out the back door, I tripped over the rug. Me 'ead 'it the edge of the door and I fell down the steps into the yard. It dain't 'alf 'urt. And it were all me gran's fault!"

"We've just seen your gran, Baz," said the Professor. "Have you got her false teeth?"

A broad impish grin spread across Baz's bruised face.

"Yeah. They was on the table so I pinched 'em to get me own back."

He fumbled in his trouser pocket, pulled out a pair of disgusting-looking top and bottom dentures, and displayed them on the palm of his hand where they sat grinning at us.

"You shouldn't have done that Baz," said Georgie. "Your gran can't eat her breakfast without her false teeth."

"They don't fit her proper, anyway 'cus she's always pullin' 'em out and moanin' that they make 'er mouth 'urt," he replied. "Then she sticks 'em in the middle of the table. That's where I got 'em from."

Charlie started to giggle.

"When we saw your gran this morning, the middle of her face had caved in like a big hole in the road," Charlie chuckled. "She kept spitting all over us when she talked, and she looked really funny."

"Me gran don't look funny!" Baz shouted angrily, tensing his whole body and fixing Charlie with a threatening stare.

It was obvious that Baz strongly objected to Charlie poking fun at his gran. I could never understand Baz. He was for ever quarrelling and arguing with her. She stopped him from doing the things he wanted to do, and he was always playing lots of tricks on her, but if anyone else criticised her or poked fun at her, Baz would immediately fly into a rage and spring to her defence. Baz and his old gran seemed to enjoy a very strange love-hate relationship.

We persuaded Baz to go home to return his gran's false teeth to the table where he had found them, while the rest of us went to our headquarters.

We sat around on our comfortable straw seats, chatting.

"I still can't believe that Baz ruined our Operation Goliath," whined Michael, who was definitely not ready to forgive him yet.

"I think he wanted to earn himself an Order of St. George for Valour," suggested Georgie.

"I reckon he was so excited about the vicar's story that he was trying to be just like David fighting Goliath," I said.

"If we'd got a Balaclava Medal for Stupidity, Baz would have a complete row of them by now," moaned Michael.

"But he's really good at football," piped up Robbie.

"Yeah, except when his boot flies over the churchyard wall and nearly knocks the vicar out," laughed Charlie.

"I've had another idea," Michael informed us.

Everyone turned towards our leader to listen to his latest wonderful brainwave.

"You know that Balaclava Cup I bought at the jumble sale? Well, I've decided that when somebody wins the Order of St. George for Valour we'll put their name on the side of the Balaclava Cup."

"How can we do that?" asked Robbie.

"Yeah, you'd need proper tools for doing engraving," the Professor informed him.

"We don't need to engrave it. We could write the name on a little strip of paper, and then stick it onto the cup."

How did Michael manage to think up all these ideas?

"Your name will go on the Balaclava Cup then, Tommy," said Georgie, resting his hand on my shoulder.

"Yes. You're the only one with an Order of St. George," added the Professor.

At the time I had been thrilled to be awarded the brigade's top military medal for bravery, and now I was delighted that this honour was to be recorded upon our newly acquired Balaclava Cup. In his very best handwriting the Professor wrote my name on a small strip of paper which Michael stuck on to the outside of the trophy. I watched with tremendous pride as the cup bearing my name was placed on top of the tall cupboard for all to see.

When Georgie, Jimmy and I went in for dinner Mrs. Millward was studying the newspaper with an anxious expression on her face.

"Hitler's bombers have been at it again," she said with a heaving sigh. "Look at all the houses they've flattened in this street."

She held out the newspaper for us to see. There was a large picture of a mass of rubble and splintered wood where a row of houses had once been.

"Where's that?" I asked nervously, because any talk of air-raids and the destruction of houses in one of our large cities always gave me a sick feeling in the pit of my stomach. She studied the newspaper again and looked up.

"In the East End of London - near the docks," she added. "I can't understand why they don't put loads of those *baggage balloons* up in the sky to stop those German bombers, you know."

"They're barrage balloons, mum, not baggage balloons" replied Georgie with a smile. "You always say that!"

"Well I think if they had lots more of those *baggage balloons* up in the sky, then the German planes wouldn't be able to fly over here and drop their bombs, would they?" she added.

"Planes can shoot down barrage balloons, you know, mum," Georgie informed her.

"Hitler will be sending his planes over here next to drop some of that *mushroom gas* on us," she sighed. "That's terrible stuff, you know. The Germans used some of that *mushroom gas* on our chaps in the last war. It got into their eyes and on their chests. Some of the chaps were blinded and some still suffer with it now, you know."

Georgie corrected his mum again.

"Mr. Hardcastle says it's called mustard gas not mushroom gas, mum."

Georgie's mum did not seem to have even noticed that her son kept correcting her.

"It makes you wonder what's going to happen next," she muttered, as she toasted a piece of bread on a long toasting fork in front of the fire in the kitchen range. "I wouldn't be one of those *Air-raid Warders* in somewhere like London for all the tea in China."

"Mum, they're Air-Raid Wardens not Warders. Warders look after people in jail," Georgie pointed out.

"They've got a terrible job, you know, those *Air-raid Warders* – pulling dead bodies out of bombed houses and dealing with all those poor people who've lost their homes. It must be awful."

She spread a thin layer of butter onto a piece of toast and then scraped most of it off again.

"I shall be glad when this rationing's over and we don't have to bother about how much butter we put on the bread," she murmured. "We've run out of coupons for butter in all our ration books."

I was wishing that she would stop talking about air-raids and people being killed. Every time I heard or thought about the blitz I became more and more anxious about my mum and dad and my pet cat, Winston, back in Birmingham. I hoped they were still alright. I had not heard or read about any raids on Birmingham recently, and I was expecting a letter from my mum very soon. I wondered how poor old Winston was coping with it all. He had never liked loud noises. Before the war started he used to 'run a mile' if the wind blew the door shut with a loud bang. I had no idea how he would cope with bombs falling all around.

Georgie's mum began again. "Some German planes went over Brinton the other night, you know. Mrs. Clamp told me that her sister went outside and saw them as plain as anything. By all accounts your teacher, Mr. Hartley, got out his *microscope* out to have a good look at them. He said he could see all the markings on them as clear as anything through that *microscope* of his."

This time Georgie did not bother to inform his mother that it must have been a telescope rather than a microscope that Adolf had been looking through.

After I had eaten my dinner I wandered down to the Brigade headquarters alone. I did not feel very much like sitting around chatting to people. I was feeling 'down in the dumps' after all the talk of air-raids, death and destruction. How much longer was this war going to last? I remembered my dad telling me that the previous war was supposed to be over by Christmas, yet it had dragged on for four long years with the deaths of millions of people. This war had only started about a year ago. Was the fighting going to last for another three years? But, of course, it might go on even longer. I wondered what was happening at home. Was everyone alright? When we had heard those German bombers a few nights ago where were they going? I did not dare think about it any longer.

I glanced around our headquarters. Instantly I noticed Robbie's plaque on the wall and the words 'Prepare To Meet Thy God' jumped out at me. I stared at the embroidered regimental picture on the wall. If that had been made by a gunner in the Royal Artillery I wondered where he was now and what he was doing. Was he still alive? No, I was sure he must have died otherwise his picture would not have been thrown out and sent to a jumble sale.

Then my eyes alighted upon the top of the tall cupboard. Something was wrong! What had happened? Where was our Balaclava Cup with my name written on it? The Victorian vase and the Laurel and Hardy cruet set were both there, but the Balaclava Cup had gone. Perhaps Michael had hidden it inside the cupboard to keep it safe, just like they do with proper regimental silver. I jumped up, ran to the cupboard and pulled open the door. Our Brigade Cup was nowhere to be seen. I searched frantically in both rooms of our HQ, but it was no good! The Balaclava Brigade Cup had mysteriously vanished. But what could have happened to it? There was only one explanation. Somebody had invaded our headquarters again, and our precious trophy had been stolen!

Chapter 25

Trouble at School

I dashed back to the house to tell Georgie and Jimmy the bad news.

"The Balaclava Cup's missing," I cried. "I can't find it anywhere."

"Michael put it on top of the cupboard in the corner," Georgie informed me.

"But it's not there," I yelled. "I've searched for it everywhere."

We raced down to our headquarters as fast as we could and searched once more. The silver cup was nowhere to be found. One by one the others arrived, but nobody knew what had happened to it.

"I put it on top of this cupboard," insisted Michael.

"Well it ain't there now, is it?" said Robbie. "Someone must have nicked it."

"'Mad Bull' Bullivant's been here again," suggested the Professor.

"Yes. He's getting his own back on us because we tried to raid his den," suggested Georgie.

"Yeah, it's Bullivant!" said Michael with an air of finality. "We know he's discovered our HQ. He was bound to get his own back on us."

"Well, we'll just have to go there again and get it back from him," said Rosie, her hands on her hips and her mouth set in a very in a determined manner.

We all agreed that we would now have to plan another secret raid on Camp Bullivant to recover our stolen brigade treasure.

"But this time we're not taking Baz with us," insisted Michael.

The following morning I was awake early. I sat up in bed and looked across at Georgie. He was awake too.

"Why do you think Bullivant would want to pinch our silver cup," I said. "It's not made of real silver, so it isn't very valuable. Michael only paid three pence for it."

"Perhaps it's his way of getting his own back on us for trying to raid his camp," Georgie answered.

Jimmy gave a little grunt, rubbed the sleep from his eyes and yawned loudly.

"I'm tired!" he muttered.

He turned over and snuggled down under the bedclothes again. The door at the bottom of the stairs creaked open and Mrs. Millward's voice came floating up to the bedroom.

"Georgie! Jimmy! Come on otherwise you'll be late for school."

On the school bus that morning Archie Fraser was his usual objectionable self. He was sitting behind Beth and he kept annoying her. He pulled her bunches of hair, untied her ribbons, flicked soggy bits of chewed-up paper at her and crawled under the seat to steal her gas mask. Finally he put a small cigarette end from the floor of the bus down the back of her dress. Rosie was sitting next to Beth, and I heard both girls yell at him several times. On one occasion I saw Beth lash out at him. This was most unusual because normally Beth was a very placid, calm and gentle sort of person.

When we arrived at school Georgie and I joined a crowd which had gathered to watch two Brinton lads playing conkers. One was a thickset, shaven-headed, bull-necked little lad nicknamed 'Gunner', while the other was a tall, gawky, doleful-looking boy usually referred to as 'Daisy'.

"Go on, Daisy whack it!" shouted his little brother, as Gunner held out his conker at arms length.

Daisy drew back his conker and smashed it down with all his strength. This mighty shot completely missed its target, and there was a loud squeal as the conker smacked heavily against Daisy's thigh. He winced, then grimaced and hopped up and down on one leg for a few moments before composing himself to hold out his conker so that Gunner could have his turn.

"Smash it, Gunner!" yelled Baz.

The stocky little lad took careful aim and crashed his conker down with tremendous force. There was a resounding thwack and Daisy's conker cartwheeled several times on the end of its string.

"Good un, Gunner," yelled Baz.

Baz turned round to face us.

"Gunner's conker's a seventy fiver," he said. "He soaked it in vinegar and put it in the oven to make it go 'ard."

He was obviously in total awe of such a champion conker.

This time Daisy grabbed hold of his conker and inspected it anxiously. He carefully scraped his thumb nail over its hard brown skin before preparing to shoot again. This time he tried to attack his opponent's conker with a hefty sideways blow, but once again his aim was off target. As the brown missile flashed dangerously round and round near his head Daisy ducked.

"He ain't very good, is he?" muttered Robbie.

"Come on Gunner!" shouted several onlookers, who were intent on supporting the ultimate winner.

Gunner was now holding his conker above his head. He closed one eye to take aim, and delivered a shot with breathtaking force. There was a flash of chestnut brown and a terrific crack. Tiny pieces flew in every direction like small fragments of shrapnel, causing spectators to duck and cover their faces. Both contestants examined their weapons. Gunner gazed in admiration at the large gleaming reddish-brown sphere hanging on the end of his string, while Daisy stared at the naked piece of twine which hung limply from his long fingers. There was nothing at all on the end of it apart from a large lonely knot. There were loud cheers from the crowd as they realised that Gunner now had a 'seventy sixer'.

Glancing across the playground, I could see that Archie Fraser was still tormenting Beth. I could also see that Rosie kept telling him to leave her alone, but he was taking no notice. I watched as he ran behind Beth again and pushed something down the back of her dress. She squealed out loud and screamed at him.

"Leave her alone!" shrieked Rosie.

Beth began to wriggle about until a large stone slid down through her clothes and clattered onto the surface of the playground. I started to walk across the yard to offer my support to the two girls. As I approached them I heard the school hand bell clanging. I turned around to see Adolf standing by the school door with the bell in his hand. All the children in the yard were standing still and quiet. At that moment a fearful howling broke the silence. Everyone turned and stared in the direction of that noise. Archie was lying in a heap on the surface of the playground, his face in the dust, his hand clutching the back of his head.

The bell rang again and everyone walked to their class lines – all except four of us. Archie was still curled up on the ground, howling at the top of his voice, while Beth, Rosie and I were standing close by staring at him anxiously. Mrs. Jolly, his class teacher, came striding towards us to investigate.

"Whatever has happened?" she asked.

"That boy wouldn't leave Beth alone," I replied, pointing at Archie.

Mrs. Jolly bent over him. She could see that a large round lump had already started to project up through Archie's hair. She helped him to his feet and draped an arm around his shoulder.

"How did this happen?" asked Mrs Jolly, looking down at Archie's grimy tear-stained face.

"Somebody …hit me ….on the head…. with a big stone," he blubbered.

"Who threw this stone?" asked Mrs. Jolly, picking up the only one in sight.

"Archie Fraser has been annoying Beth ever since we left Stretton," I said indignantly.

"That was not what I asked you," replied Mrs. Jolly. "I asked you who threw this stone."

I was not sure who had thrown it. Beth and Rosie both looked nervous. I knew that Beth had never been in any kind of trouble before, and Rosie was very new to our school.

"I can only assume that it is one of you three who has injured Archie Fraser," the teacher said, exhibiting the stone on the palm of her hand. "Mr.

Hardcastle is not going to be very happy when he finds out about this."

I thought that was a colossal understatement.

We all stood still, staring silently at Archie who was now wailing again like an air-raid siren.

"Did you throw it?" asked Mrs Jolly curtly, staring straight at Beth.

Beth stood still, her lips tightly closed, her eyes fixed on the playground. Suddenly she put her head in her hands and started to sob. I thought Archie's teacher looked anything but jolly at that particular moment.

"But it was his fault really, Miss," I protested, desperate to protect both girls.

"It was the fault of whoever threw this stone," insisted Mrs. Jolly. "Now who threw it?"

Nobody spoke up. I knew Mr. Hardcastle viewed stone throwing in school extremely seriously. We were constantly being told how dangerous it was to throw stones at other people. Perhaps Mr. Hardcastle was more aware of the dangers than most, since he had lost an eye during the previous war. I glanced at both girls again, and then at Mrs. Jolly. I had no idea who had thrown it.

"Come on! I am waiting!" exclaimed Mrs. Jolly fiercely, and she looked at each of us in turn for signs of guilt.

I glanced at Beth who was still crying. Her face was blanched, and she looked petrified. I looked again at Rosie. She was fidgeting uneasily. Rosie had no idea how fearsome Mr. Hardcastle could be when he was angry. I could not stand by and watch either of those two girls get into such terrible trouble. Instantly I felt an overwhelming urge to speak up.

"It was me, Miss," I called out. "I was the one who threw it!"

Chapter 26

A Letter from Home

Mrs. Jolly stared at me.

"While I see to this boy you can go and stand outside Mr. Hardcastle's room, Thomas Dennis," she instructed. "I do not know what he's going to say when he finds out that you have injured someone by hitting them on the head with a large stone."

Reluctantly I shuffled off to present myself outside the Head's door. Never before had I been sent to Mr. Hardcastle's room in disgrace. As I wandered unhappily across the playground I was feeling very apprehensive, for I kept reminding myself that stone-throwing was one of Brinton National School's deadliest sins. Moreover, I knew that Mr. Hardcastle was a terrifying figure when he was angry. As I arrived outside his room, trembling like a leaf in a gale force wind, I felt sure that I was in for a good whacking with his cane. I waited anxiously by his door.

As I shuffled nervously from one foot to the other I heard his loud voice.

"Yes, who is it?"

I plucked up courage and stepped inside, still quaking in my shoes. Mr. Hardcastle was sitting behind his huge oak desk, and he was writing something in a large leather-bound writing book. A long thin cane lay on top of the desk in front of him. After a few seconds he stopped writing and raised his head. He seemed to be looking in my direction, his pen hovering in mid air above the page.

"Please sir, Mrs. Jolly sent me to stand here," I stuttered.

He said nothing, but lowered his head slowly and continued to write. The pen nib squeaked and scratched noisily across the page, and the large round clock on the wall ticked deafeningly. My eyes were riveted on that cane, and I was beginning to regret that I had decided to take the blame for throwing that stone at Archie Fraser.

Eventually Mr. Hardcastle paused again, his pen suspended once more above the book. He seemed to be staring at the page of writing in front of him.

"And why has she sent you here?" he said, without even looking up.

"I didn't mean to hit him, sir," I said nervously. "It was an accident."

"Hit him? Who did you hit and where did you hit him?"

"Archie Fraser, sir. On the back of the head," I replied.

"And how did you manage to do that?"

"I accidentally threw a stone, sir," I stammered.

"Oh, I see!" he exclaimed loudly. "You threw a stone - accidentally!"

He raised his head, and I was sure that one of his eyes was staring straight at me. I looked down at the floor, for I could not bring myself to look at him.

"And how did you manage to throw a stone accidentally, may I ask?" he continued.

I tried to explain that Archie Fraser had been annoying a girl in his class. I told him that Beth had been very upset because he would not stop tormenting her, and I explained how Rosie and I had tried to stop him. I then described how he had put a large stone down the back of her dress, and when it had fallen onto the playground I had picked it up and thrown it after him, not intending to hit him. I assured him that I would never throw a stone at anybody, deliberately intending to hit them.

"I am very surprised at you, Thomas Dennis. I have always thought of you as a very sensible boy. But that was an extremely silly thing to do, was it not?"

"Yes Mr. Hardcastle," I agreed.

"I am most disappointed to think that you have behaved so foolishly."

"Yes, sir."

Roland Bond

"You know that throwing stones is extremely dangerous and strictly forbidden in this school."

"Yes, sir."

"However, I can see that you are very sorry that you have caused an injury to this boy. I am also prepared to accept that it was probably not your intention to hit him with that stone. Since you have never before been in any trouble in this school, I shall give you the benefit of the doubt on this occasion."

"Thank you, sir," I answered gratefully. "I am very sorry."

Mr. Hardcastle then delivered a very stern lecture about the dangers of throwing stones, emphasising that he did not expect me to be sent to his room ever again for such reckless and potentially dangerous behaviour.

At morning playtime Georgie was very eager to receive a detailed report about what had happened in Mr. Hardcastle's room. As I was talking to him Rosie came across and joined us. Her black hair was gleaming in the sunlight and her dark eyes were flashing.

"Why did you do that?" she asked sharply, fixing me with a dagger-like stare.

"Do what?" I asked.

"Why did you say that it was you that threw that stone?" she snapped. "I was just about to own up."

I was completely stunned by her reaction.

"I don't know," I answered. "I suppose I thought you were new and ….."

She interrupted me.

"I am quite capable of looking after myself, you know!" she said very firmly. "My dad has taught me to do that. I don't need you or anyone else to protect me!"

She turned haughtily and flounced away, her pony tail bouncing as she walked. I was feeling very upset that she had reacted in this way. I felt just as badly hurt as if she had taken a running jump and kicked me in the teeth.

When Jimmy, Georgie and I walked into the cottage at the end of the afternoon, Mrs. Millward informed me that there was a letter waiting for me. I picked it up and glanced at the envelope. I realised instantly that it was from my mum. Impatiently I ripped open the envelope and began to read the contents. My eyes raced over each line in turn. I stood totally motionless, my fingers gripping the paper tightly and my eyes staring blankly at the writing in front of me. I read it again and again, my hands trembling as I clung on to the paper. Instantly I began to feel an awful sinking feeling in the pit of my stomach. Surely this could not be true! There must be some mistake!

Chapter 27

Undercover Expert

Clutching the letter, I hurried upstairs and sat on my bed. I read it again and again very slowly, trying to take in every word. It read as follows:-

My dear Tommy,

I am writing this short note to let you know that your dad and I are alright. You might have heard that the German bombers raided the Dunlop factory in broad daylight a few days ago. Your dad was at work at the time but he is OK. They missed the factory but some of the bombs landed on the Dunlop sports ground. Unfortunately one or two bombs also landed in our road. Lots of our windows were blown in by the blast but a couple of stray bombs scored direct hits on houses further up the street. Poor Joey Sanderson's house has been absolutely flattened by the blast. Mr. Sanderson was at work at the time and Joey was at school. But they think his mum and his little sister were probably in the house. They are still missing, believed killed. The men are there now digging in the rubble as I write. Mrs. Talbot, the old lady I sometimes visit at No. 47, has also been killed and apparently they've recovered her body. Three of houses where Mrs. Talbot lived have been totally demolished. That raid was really nasty and we didn't have very much of a warning before the bombs started falling. I went down into the shelter as soon as the sirens went off but the scream of the bombs and the noise of the explosions were quite awful. I'm afraid Winston was out at the time and we haven't seen him since. I expect he ran away somewhere to hide but he'll probably return when he's ready. I will write to you again as soon as he comes back home. Please don't worry about us because we are fine. I doubt if our road will be hit again. They say lightning never strikes twice in the same place. The same probably goes for bombs as well! Your dad and I hope you are keeping well and that you are behaving yourself. Give our regards to Mr. & Mrs. Millward.

Roland Bond

*Your ever loving
Mum and Dad.*

Poor Joey Sanderson! He is one of my very best friends at home, and his mum was a really nice person. Joey and I used to play in his back garden with his little sister, a pretty happy little girl with a mass of golden curls. I could not believe that Joey's mum and sister had both been killed like that! And poor Winston! Ever since I had left Birmingham I had been worried about him. I knew he would be scared stiff if there was a bombing raid. I just hoped that he was hiding safely somewhere, and that he would go back home soon. And I could not believe what mum had said about old Mrs. Talbot – what a way for a harmless old lady to end her life, blown up by a huge German bomb!

I was feeling very angry and extremely upset. What right did those German pilots have to fly over our country, dropping their bombs on the homes of ordinary innocent people! The stark reality of this war was beginning to dawn on me. Now I knew that enemy bombs did not just fall on unknown faceless people – nameless folk who were simply numbers that we heard about. I was suddenly aware that they could kill real people whom I knew and who lived around me in my own street at home. My mum was right! Fighting *is* stupid. I wondered how much longer this awful senseless war was going to last.

I was feeling pretty miserable because this had been one of the worst days of my life! For the first time since I started at Brinton National School I had got myself into serious trouble, and had been sent to Mr. Hardcastle's room. After I had taken the blame for the stone-throwing incident to protect the two girls, Rosie had responded by being horrible to me. I had just heard that Winston, my cat, had gone missing from home during an air-raid. And worst of all, my best friend's mother and sister and my mum's friend, old Mrs. Talbot, had all been killed by German bombs. I did not think that it was possible for a day to be much worse than that!

I climbed into the look-out post in the apple tree and sat down. Whenever I was feeling miserable I always felt that things did not look quite so bad when I was high up looking out between the leafy twigs and branches of that tree. Eventually Georgie and Jimmy clambered up to join me.

"Why did you say you threw that stone at Archie Fraser?" asked Jimmy. "I knew it wasn't you 'cus I saw Rosie chuck it."

"I don't know why I said it," I answered. "I just did."

"It was all Archie Fraser's fault really," continued Jimmy.

"I wish he'd go back to where he came from," muttered Georgie.

I remained silent.

Suddenly Georgie knelt up and stared towards the Jones's cottage.

"Crikey!" he exclaimed.

"What's the matter?" asked his brother.

"Can you see something inside Wilma's window?" he replied.

Jimmy peered out through the foliage.

"I know what *that* looks like," he said.

I knelt up to have a look. Wilma's scullery window was open and something just inside the window on the ledge was glinting in the light of the sinking sun.

"Are you thinking what I'm thinking?" said Georgie.

"Yes, I think it could be," I replied.

"Well, somehow we'll have to make sure," my friend added.

We climbed down from the tree and went off in search of Baz.

"Baz, can you come and do a little job for us?" asked Georgie.

"What d'you want?" he said.

"We want you to creep up Wilma's garden path and see what's on the window ledge in her scullery," Georgie told him.

"But don't tell Michael that we've asked you to do it," I added. "He says you're not allowed to carry out any more special missions."

"OK," he replied.

We returned to our HQ and, full of enthusiasm, Baz embarked upon his spying mission. It was not very long before he returned.

"I've seen it," he reported. "It's our silver cup. I tried to grab it, but then I 'eard Wilma comin' so I 'ad to duck down quick so she dain't see me. Then I nipped round the corner."

"Well done, Baz," said Georgie, patting the little fellow on the back.

I was still feeling fed up and pretty miserable. To add to all my other problems Archie Fraser had stolen our Balaclava Cup with my name written on it. I got up and went outside to be on my own for a few minutes. A lot had happened during that day, and I needed a little more time to take it all in.

I had been standing on the garden path for a few minutes when I heard footsteps running towards me. Rosie came round the corner.

"Hi Tommy," she said very cheerily. "Are you alright?"

I did not answer her.

"I've been thinking!" she continued. "I'm very sorry that I was so horrible to you today, after you'd told Mrs. Jolly you'd thrown that stone at Archie Fraser. I shouldn't have said those things to you. I think it was really nice of you to take the blame for me, Tommy."

"That's alright," I mumbled without even looking at her.

"I know that you did it to stop me from getting into trouble with the Mr. Hardcastle, and I think what you did was really brave. I don't know anybody else that would have done that for me."

She grabbed hold of my arm and gave it a gentle squeeze. Now that she felt like that I was feeling a whole lot better. I could not help thinking that everything I had done to protect her had been worthwhile and, given the same situation again in the future, I knew that I would protect her.

One by one the other brigade members arrived. We went inside our headquarters to discuss how we were going to retrieve our Balaclava Cup.

"I can't believe that nasty little creature has had the nerve to come in here and pinch our cup," Michael said.

"We've got to get it back," said the Professor. "That's our brigade treasure."

"There's only one person who can do it without being seen," argued Georgie. "We've got to let Baz go and get it."

"No!" shouted Michael. "He's already spoilt one important mission. I'm not going to let him mess up another one."

"I won't muck it up," pleaded Baz, who was eager to make amends.

"What happens if you get caught?" argued Michael snappily.

"Wilma will probably get out her wand and turn him into a slug or a frog," laughed Charlie. "On second thoughts, that might make him look loads better!"

Charlie put his head between his knees and chuckled noisily.

"I think Baz *could* do it," I said.

Georgie, Jimmy, Beth and Robbie all agreed.

"But what if she recognises him?" said Michael. "The whole brigade will get the blame and Wilma will go mad at us."

"That's a good point," said Georgie. "Everybody in Stretton would recognise Baz straight away."

Up to that point Rosie had said nothing at all, but now she joined the conversation.

"Why doesn't he go in disguise? Then even if he's spotted she won't know who it is."

What a brilliant idea! Why couldn't I have thought of that! Now I was convinced that Rosie was almost as clever as the Professor.

Everybody looked across at Michael.

"It will have to be a good disguise then, 'cus if Wilma recognises him she'll know we've put him up to it," our leader said.

"But if Baz's disguise is really good," argued the Professor, "then it won't matter if Wilma does catch sight of him because she won't know who it is."

Thanks to Rosie we had come up with a wonderful scheme! An undercover operation carried out in disguise! That was the perfect plan for getting our Balaclava Brigade Silver Cup back.

"What's a 'disguise' mean?" asked Baz, looking puzzled.

"It means that you change how you look - just like a secret undercover agent - so that nobody knows it's you," explained the Professor.

"D'you mean you want me to get dressed up like a secret agent?" asked Baz, his eyes widening.

"Yes, just like a very special operations commando," butted in Georgie.

"Yeah *I* can do that!" exclaimed Baz eagerly, " 'cus I'm a hexpert."

I am certain that Baz could picture himself dressed in khaki with his balaclava helmet over his head, and his face camouflaged. He was so thrilled at the prospect of being a secret agent that he was jumping up and down. It also looked as if Michael had warmed to Rosie's little plan.

"I know what we'll do!" Michael exclaimed. "I'll sort out a disguise. Leave it to me. I'll meet you all in here tomorrow evening after tea."

The following evening everybody gathered inside our brigade HQ, and Michael appeared carrying a large leather suitcase, while Baz was so excited that he could hardly keep still.

"I've checked to make sure that Wilma's scullery window is open," said Michael, "so we'll be able to get our cup back tonight."

"I'll make sure I get it!" said Baz confidently. " 'cus I'm a hexpert commando."

"Right Baz, you come in here with me and I'll get you ready," ordered Michael, grabbing hold of Baz by the arm.

He pushed the little lance-corporal inside the pig-house part of our headquarters, and pulled the piece of black-out curtain across the doorway.

The rest of us sat around trying to picture Baz in his secret agent's costume.

Suddenly we heard Baz's voice protesting loudly from behind the curtain.

"I ain't wearing that!" he shouted.

"You do want to carry out this mission, don't you?" shouted our Colonel.

There was another prolonged period of silence apart from the shuffling of feet and the rustling of clothes inside the pig-house.

Suddenly a second loud cry of protest rang out.

"I ain't wearin' that and I ain't carryin' that thing," Baz yelled.

"Oh yes you are," answered Michael, "otherwise you can't go on this secret undercover job."

All went quiet again. It was not long there was another violent outburst from Baz.

"I ain't wearin' them, I'm tellin' you!" he bawled.

"Yes you are!" shouted Michael. "You do want to be a secret agent, don't you?"

What was going on in there?

There was more shuffling around and a constant rustling of clothing. A few seconds later Baz shrieked out again.

"I ain't 'avin' any of that stuff on me face!"

"Stand still, Baz!" bawled our leader, who seemed to be growing increasingly impatient with our undercover lance-corporal.

It sounded as if Michael was smothering Baz's face with dirt or coal dust so that he would not easily be recognised. But why was Baz protesting?

Suddenly the curtain was thrust aside and Michael appeared. He turned round and urged Baz to follow him. Our little undercover expert seemed to be refusing to emerge.

"Come on, Baz," ordered Michael, as he looked back into the pig-house

"I ain't comin' out!" replied a sulky voice from inside.

"Come on, Baz! Let's see what you look like," called Beth.

"Let's have a look at you, Baz," cried Charlie.

There was a little hesitant fumbling with the curtain and slowly it was pushed aside. From inside the pig-house a small hunched figure emerged very slowly. Baz now stood before us, staring at the floor and looking decidedly uncomfortable. As soon as we caught sight of him pandemonium broke out among the ranks. Everyone had erupted into uncontrollable fits of laughter.

Chapter 28

Mission Accomplished

We howled and roared at the sight of our little lance-corporal, and rolled about on our seats. We were completely helpless! Baz was standing before us, an angry expression on his face, his head hung low, his eyes staring at the floor.

He was dressed in one of Beth's short cotton frocks which was decorated with printed white daisies against a pale pink background. Over it he wore a bright pink woollen cardigan. Short white ankle socks and little black shoes with ankle straps took care of his feet. His stubbly head was shrouded in a white bonnet from which hung two pigtails made out of plaited yellow wool. They were draped tastefully over both shoulders, and tied at the ends with two pink ribbons. His pale grey complexion had been brought to life by the addition of some rosy red cheeks, and in his arms he was cradling one of Beth's dolls.

When the laughter had subsided Baz looked up.

"What's so funny?" he asked, his eyes darting around at us all in turn.

That unnecessary question prompted another outburst of spontaneous and rowdy laughter.

"What have you got on underneath there?" giggled Charlie, stretching forward a finger to lift the hem of Baz's frock.

"Get off!" yelled Baz angrily as he backed away. "You ain't lookin'!"

"You look really lovely, Baz," taunted Charlie with a glint in his eye.

"I ain't goin' out lookin' like this," Baz announced grumpily, as he threw Beth's doll down onto the floor. "I look stupid!"

"Well you can't go on this mission if you don't go in disguise," insisted Michael. "We're going to make sure that nobody knows who you are."

"You needn't worry, Baz," said Georgie. "Nobody would ever know it was you because *that* is a brilliant disguise."

He turned his face away towards the wall, and stifled a giggle.

"Yeah, Baz" said Charlie, "It's so good I'd even have you for my girlfriend," and then he put his head in his hands and shrieked with laughter.

Baz thought for a few seconds before bending down to pick up his doll. As he did so the ragged grey bottoms of his own short trouser legs were clearly visible beneath the hemline of his little short dress.

"Baz, you can't wear your own trousers under there," I cried. "We can see them."

"Well I ain't wearin' no girls' pants!" he shouted.

"I think they would suit you," added Charlie, giggling and burying his head in his hands again.

"I *ain't* wearing no girl's pants," repeated Baz more emphatically.

"I've got some white football shorts at home," said Jimmy, "You can wear them."

He ran off to fetch them.

Finally Baz was ready to undertake his secret mission. We had worked out an excellent plan. Rosie would climb into the look-out post from where she could see Wilma's scullery window and give Baz the necessary hand signals. Baz's route had been worked out so that Wilma would have little chance of spotting him. We did not have long to wait to see if our plan was good enough, for the whole operation worked like clockwork. Baz approached Wilma's back garden via the road and then waited around the corner of her cottage wall. Crouching high in the apple tree, Rosie saw Baz waiting by Wilma's gable end. Since our sergeant-major could see no movement in the scullery she reached through the foliage and gave Baz the 'thumbs up' sign. He darted along the wall to the scullery window, clambered up on a waste water pipe, put his hand through the open window, grabbed the Balaclava Cup and darted back the way he had come. Baz had carried out the whole operation in seconds just like a real commando.

I did not realise it until Baz came back but that was not the end of the matter. Apparently, as our little undercover agent dashed onto the pavement, clutching the cup in one hand and Beth's doll in the other, he bumped into his next door neighbour who was returning home from the village shop with a bag full of shopping. At first she looked at him in a very strange manner.

Then in a bright and cheery voice she said, "Oh, hello, Barry! Going to a fancy dress party, are we? You make a very pretty little girl, I must say."

Chapter 29

Apples, Gas Masks and Blackberries

When Baz joined us in our HQ he was looking extremely fed up with life.

"I ain't never gonna dress up in girls' things no more," he vowed.

"Well it was worth it, Baz, 'cus we've got our Brigade Cup back," said Jimmy.

"If that woman next door tells me gran I've bin wearin' girls' things she'll go mad," whined Baz.

Charlie sniggered and, imitating the high-pitched voice of Baz's next door neighbour, he said, "I saw your Barry today and he was dressed up as a little girl with pigtails and he was carrying a little girl's dolly."

"Leave him alone, Charlie," I said. "Baz did really well and now we've got our cup back, thanks to him."

Georgie suddenly changed the subject.

"I've just remembered. Our mum wants us to pick some apples from the trees so that she can store them away for the winter. She says we must make sure that we handle them carefully, because they won't keep if they're bruised."

"We could pick some apples for ourselves," suggested Jimmy. "And we could store them in boxes in the pig-house. It's cold enough in there."

"Yeah and then we'd have our own store of apples," I said. "They'd last us for ages."

"I doubt if they'll last 'til next week if Baz gets his hands on them – especially those cookers," laughed Charlie.

Every October Georgie's mum gathered apples from their trees to put them into store for the winter months. Eating and cooking apples were wrapped individually in newspaper, and then placed in boxes to be stored low down on the cold stone floor of her cool pantry. Put away like that they would keep until just after Christmas, so that the Millward family had a supply of eating and cooking apples for several months every year.

Everyone in the brigade agreed to help with the apple picking. We divided ourselves into two squads, one to collect the eaters in Mrs. Millward's large clothes basket and the other to fill a large tin bath with cookers. We allocated Baz to the group picking the eaters for obvious reasons. There was no way we could face the possibility of him being sick again. When Georgie's mum had chosen all the apples she needed she told us that we could have the rest. We carefully wrapped our apples in newspaper and placed them in the boxes which were left over from our apple selling trip round the village. Then we placed them on the cold stone floor in the corner of our pig-house.

The remainder of our school week passed without incident, but unfortunately it seemed to drag by very slowly. When Friday afternoon came Adolf, our teacher, said that he would carry on reading a story called *'Great Expectations'* which was written by a man called Charles Dickens. It was an exciting story about a little orphan lad called Pip, who lived with his bossy sister and her husband, Joe, the village blacksmith. The last time he had read the story to us we had reached the part of the book where Pip was alone in the churchyard, taking comfort from being near the grave of his dead parents. As he was looking at the inscriptions on their tombstone a rough-looking convict, dressed in rags and with large iron shackles attached to his ankles, suddenly sprang out from behind one of the gravestones and grabbed hold of him. We were dying to know what happened next.

"I am going to continue reading the story about Pip in the churchyard now," announced Adolf.

There was a flurry of excitement. Our teacher opened the cupboard, took out the book and began to flick through its pages. Having found the correct page, he was about to continue with the story when Mr. Hardcastle thrust open the door and poked his head into the room.

"Everyone must go into the Hall immediately, taking their gas masks with them," he ordered. "There is to be a gas mask drill."

He closed the door and disappeared as quickly as he had arrived.

"Oh, sir, do we have to go to the Hall?" we all cried. "We want to hear some more of that story about Pip in the churchyard."

At regular intervals each term, the entire school was subjected to a gas mask drill, because Mr. Hardcastle thought it vital that we should all have regular practice at putting on our gas masks quickly in case the Germans mounted a surprise gas attack. Because he had seen the terrible effects of German gas in the trenches during the First World War he knew better than most how important our gas masks were. On such occasions Mr. Hardcastle would drill the whole school with military precision.

Our class was marched reluctantly into the Hall by Adolf and, when the entire school was assembled in rows, Mr Hardcastle stood at the front and began.

"Now children, put your gas mask boxes on the floor in front of you with your gas masks still inside them. Your gas mask is a very important piece of equipment. One day your life might depend on it. Hitler will not wait around, you know, while you search for your gas mask or while you spend half the day trying to put it on. Speed is of the utmost importance. Does everybody understand?"

"Yes Mr. Hardcastle," we all chanted.

"Very good! Now, when I blow my whistle, you will all open your boxes, put your gas masks on and, as soon as you have finished, you will sit up straight with arms folded. Remember! You put your chin into it first and then pull the straps over the top of your head. I am going to time you with my watch. Are you all ready?"

The entire school repeated the chorus, "Yes, Mr. Hardcastle."

Our headmaster took a huge pocket watch from his waistcoat pocket and blew a shrill blast on his whistle, whereupon the Hall suddenly erupted into a frenzied hive of activity. Boxes were flung open; gas masks were snatched out and straps were dragged on over every head. Soon we were all sitting up straight with our arms folded, apart from one flustered little boy who was still struggling to disentangle his gas mask straps.

"You boy!" yelled the Headmaster. "If we were in the middle of a real gas attack you would be dead!"

"Please sir, I can't get me gas mask sorted out," stammered the young lad.

"That's probably because you left it in a mess the last time you took it off," shouted Mr. Hardcastle.

Adolf was now threading his way along the row of feet and respirator boxes to assist the troubled youngster.

"Now you can all understand why it is important to place your gas mask carefully in your box ready for the next time you need to use it."

A muffled indistinct mumbling noise struggled to emerge from inside every respirator as the assembled company attempted to reply.

"There is little point in having your gas mask with you if you are unable to put it on quickly," the Head added tersely, staring at the little boy who was holding his gas mask up in front of his face.

Meanwhile Adolf had managed to unravel the boy's tangled straps, and was now tiptoeing back along the line towards his seat at the side of the Hall.

As the guilty lad belatedly hauled on his mask the rest of us were sitting in silence, staring at Mr. Hardcastle through large oval glassy eye pieces which were slowly misting up, our faces encased in foul-smelling black rubber attached to large protruding snouts, which resembled tin cans with holes bodged in the bottom. The faces around me looked more like the magnified features of an army of grotesque giant insects.

I hated gas mask drill in school. Firstly, we were forced to sit for what seemed like hours inside the stuffy school Hall, wearing our gas masks which felt extremely hot and smelly; secondly, with my gas mask on I usually found it difficult to breathe; thirdly, the eye piece always misted up so that I could not see very well; and finally, there was always the danger that one might accidentally blow inside the rubber mask, thus creating a loud rasping extremely rude noise as the air reverberated against one's cheeks in its attempt to escape from the tight-fitting rubber walls.

Whilst we would never deliberately do that in school, it had not taken us boys very long to discover that enormous fun could be had by making such rude noises when nobody was about. Sometimes if we had missed the bus home from school we would walk back through Stretton woods, and we would amuse ourselves by holding rude noise competitions. Everyone would put on his respirator to see who could make the loudest and most revolting noise possible by blowing very hard inside his mask. As every rude noise was blown, we would dissolve into fits of laughter. Despite the fact that he was very small Baz was our champion rude noise maker. He could usually make the loudest, the longest and the rudest noise imaginable. We all knew that we must never play this game at school, for gas mask drill at Brinton National School was a very serious business. We would never think of fooling around in such a manner. Any child who blew loud raspberry noises into his gas mask in school would certainly suffer the worst possible punishment.

"We will try again," said our headmaster from the front of the Hall. "Take off your gas masks and place them inside your boxes."

Everyone did as instructed, and we all sat up straight once more with arms folded, elbows stretching up into the air. Mr. Hardcastle put his whistle to his lips and blew a loud shrill blast once more. Once again there was a desperate flurry of activity. This time everyone carried out the task with tremendous speed and great efficiency.

"Excellent! That was much better," said Mr. Hardcastle as he wandered up and down in front of the school, his face confirming that he was extremely pleased with our efforts.

No sooner had our Headmaster finished speaking than a long, extremely loud raspberry sound echoed throughout the Hall. Immediately every respirator snout and steamed-up glassy eye piece turned in the direction of the culprit.

"Who made that revolting sound?" bellowed our Headmaster, his cheeks flushed with anger and his eyes bulging.

A forest of arms pointed at one particular little lad, and this was accompanied by a chorus of muffled mumblings.

"Stand up that boy!" shouted the furious Head, his hand waving about in a vague manner.

A little lad scrambled to his feet looking like an overgrown ant with an outsized head. His socks were crumpled round his ankles and there was a huge hole in the front of his jumper. It was Baz.

"Why did you make that disgusting sound?" demanded the irate Head.

A jumble of faint murmurings rushed around inside Baz's respirator, vainly trying to find a means of escape.

"I can't hear you, boy! Remove your gas mask!" yelled the Headmaster.

Baz did as he was told. His pale grey face was vaguely visible through my misty eye piece. He seemed a little confused and nervous.

"Now would you mind telling me why you made that disgraceful noise?" Mr. Hardcastle asked again.

"I 'ad an itch up me nose, Mr. 'Ardcastle," replied Baz uneasily, his grimy fingers clutching the straps of his respirator which dangled by his side.

"You had an itch up your nose, did you?"

"Yes, Mr. 'Ardcastle," replied Baz. "I couldn't scratch it so I tried blowin' on it, Mr. 'Ardcastle."

"You were not able to scratch your nose so you blew on it!" the Head repeated. "I have heard many excuses in my time but that explanation beats them all! Go and stand by my door, boy! Now!"

Baz began to make his way to the side of the Hall, his stubbly head hanging low, his feet tripping over an assortment of feet, legs and gas mask boxes as he tried to pick his way along the line. As he left the Hall we all knew that this was not

Baz's day. He was bound to suffer the ultimate punishment.

That evening after tea we gathered inside our headquarters, and Georgie told us that his mum needed some blackberries to make blackberry and apple jam.

"Will you come blackberry picking with me," asked Georgie.

"Where are you going?" I asked.

"Brinton Copse is the best place for blackberries round here," he replied. "We always go there 'cus there's loads of bushes and the blackberries are great big juicy ones."

"Yes I'll come," I replied.

Instantly every brigade member agreed to go with us. We gathered together an assortment of tins and jars for collecting the blackberries and, armed with sticks to push away the prickly brambles, we set off across Blore's field. Our destination was Brinton Copse, that dense patch of bramble bushes renowned locally for its large succulent fruit. Having finally reached this blackberry paradise, we fanned out among the bushes to start picking.

We had been gathering blackberries for some time when Baz came dashing through the undergrowth. His tin was empty but around his mouth were the tell-tale signs that once again he had been gorging himself on the fruits of Mother Nature.

"I've just seen Bullivant," he panted. "And he's comin' this way."

"Is there anybody else with him?" asked the Professor urgently.

"Yes, he's got them two big uns with him," he replied.

"We'll have to split up and head for home then," said Michael. "We can't stay here or else we'll get caught."

I was stretching up, trying to pick an enormous blackberry, a delicious-looking juicy specimen at the very top of the bush. As I reached up on tip toes to get it, the sleeve of my jumper became hooked on a bramble branch with huge curving prickles. With my jar in one hand and my stick tucked under my arm I was having difficulty unhooking my sleeve. I glanced around. All my friends had disappeared. I dropped my stick and tried to free myself.

"There's that Brummie kid!" yelled a rough deep voice some distance away.

I glanced up. 'Mad Bull' Bullivant's huge ginger-haired mate had just come into view. Scarface and Bullivant were close behind. I tried to yank my sleeve away from the bush but it would not budge. My arm was caught fast. As I glanced behind me once more I could see that Bullivant and his two thugs were heading straight for me. Now I was in trouble!

Chapter 30

The Churchyard Refuge

I struggled desperately to free myself, wondering if I was going to be able to get away. But no matter how hard I tried I could not release my jumper from that bramble. Finally, in sheer desperation, I jerked my arm downwards violently, and my jar of blackberries fell. At least my arm was now free, although a long broken woollen thread was dangling from the elbow of my sleeve. At my feet lay my stick, my empty jam jar and all my blackberries which were strewn around in the grass. Abandoning everything, I turned and ran as fast as I could, trampling and leaping through the undergrowth. As I charged headlong through that copse my legs were scratched and smarting. I could hear the three thugs stampeding after me, bellowing and roaring like a herd of wild elephants.

Emerging onto the main road, I glanced over my shoulder. I could not see my pursuers, but I could hear them as they shouted instructions to each another within the copse. Instantly I looked around for somewhere to hide. Across the road, beside our school, was the old parish church, almost buried among its ancient tombstones. I sprinted across the road and darted into the churchyard, taking refuge behind a large round-topped moss-covered gravestone. Peeping from behind this large slab of rock, I saw the lumbering trio pause in front of the churchyard gates. They were looking around, obviously wondering which way I had gone. After a brief discussion, Bullivant sloped off to look for me around the buildings in the school yard; the ginger-haired one went back across the road to continue searching the copse; and that colossal hulk, Scarface, came shambling into the churchyard, a long stout stick in his huge fist.

My mind flashed back to the story which Adolf had been reading to us about Pip in the churchyard. I was now faced with a similar situation. Here I was among the churchyard tombstones, with an ugly rough-looking fiend nearby. In the story by Charles Dickens, Pip had been grabbed as he rested among the graves. I was hoping that the same fate did not await me!

I crawled from gravestone to gravestone, slithering along on my stomach and my elbows in the long grass, and trying to keep as far away as possible from the brute. But I was finding it difficult to keep track of him. Now I decided that it would be unwise to keep dodging about from grave to grave, for the more I lifted my head the greater would be the chance that he would spot me. Then, out of the corner of my eye, I noticed a gigantic table-top tomb, rectangular in shape, its walls built of large slabs of purple-blue slate. This vast monument, which I knew would provide a much larger barrier behind which I could hide, was near the church wall. I slithered across to it, unaware of exactly where Scarface was. I heard a loud thwack some distance away as my enemy struck the top of one of the gravestones with his stick. He was doing everything he could to frighten me into submission. I was absolutely petrified.

As I crept along the side of this large rectangular slate monument I noticed that the end panel had collapsed and was lying on the ground. I peered inside the tomb. I could see nothing, for the interior was pitch black. Instantly I realised that this enormous slate box would provide an excellent hiding place. But what was inside there?

I peered into the black interior of this structure again. No, I could not possibly crawl inside somebody's tomb. I shrank back at the very thought of it. What terrors might await me inside that place? Perhaps within that impenetrable blackness there was a deep hole into which I would plunge. What would I find at the bottom of that pit? I shuddered to think what might be lurking there. All kinds of grotesque thoughts kept flashing through my mind as I continued to stare into that empty void. Suddenly I heard another loud thump as the huge fellow whacked the top of another tombstone.

I was in no doubt that he was getting much nearer. I would have to do something very quickly. Either I must pluck up courage and crawl inside that tomb or stay outside and run the risk of being discovered. Without giving it another thought, I began to wriggle inside the tomb feet first. To my surprise there was no hole into which I could fall and, as I slithered cautiously away from the light, I felt nothing but cool damp soil and small stones against my hands and knees. Backing up to the far end of this hollow monument, I curled into a tight ball and lay perfectly still. An unpleasant dank musty smell pervaded the place. I held my breath and lay there hoping that my pursuer would pass by. I was now so overcome with fear that I was trembling, my stomach was churning, my mouth felt dry and I could feel my heart thumping.

Suddenly there was an ear-splitting crash above my head like that of a bomb exploding. That deafening noise took me completely by surprise, and it was so loud that it made me wince, grit my teeth, and close my eyes. I knew instantly that Scarface had smashed his stick upon the slate top of the very tomb where I was hiding. After a few seconds I opened my eyes and peered out towards the light. Now I could see an enormous pair of muddy boots standing at the end of the tomb. I hardly dared breathe.

Very slowly those boots began to move, and then the person wearing them bent down. An ugly stubbly face appeared at the end of the tomb, and two fierce piercing eyes peered in at me. I could see the jagged scar running down his cheek. I had been discovered!

"Why did I decide to crawl inside this place?" I thought to myself.

What was I to do now? I was trapped and this time there was no escape. I was completely at this monster's mercy.

Chapter 31

The Magnificent Cockerel

I closed my eyes and waited for the huge ruffian to make the next move. I was wondering what I would do if he crawled inside this tomb to drag me out, or if he started to poke and prod me with his long stick. Then I heard another movement. I opened my eyes and peered towards the light again. The boots had disappeared. All I could see was the stone wall of the church and the blades of grass at the end of the tomb gently swaying in the autumn breeze.

I heard another loud thwack as Scarface smashed his stick down upon another gravestone nearby. That noise seemed a little further away. Where exactly was he now? Was he walking away? Had he not seen me? Then I remembered that, when I had bent down to peer inside this empty slate box, I could see nothing but an intense blackness, as if I was peering into a bottomless pit. It dawned upon me that I had been able to see him because he was outside in the sunlight, but he could not see me, curled up at the far end of that pitch-black enclosed space.

I continued to lie there too scared to move. I was sure that Bullivant would go on searching because he was not the sort of person to give up easily. So there I remained, concealed within that ancient chamber. I am not sure for how long I lay there but it seemed like an eternity. I lay perfectly motionless, cramped and frightened, wondering whose final resting place lay beneath me. Whoever it was, I was very grateful for their hospitality. At last I plucked up courage, crawled towards the light and peeped out cautiously. Nobody was in sight, and all was quiet apart from a few birds chirping and a horse and cart clip-clopping along the road through the village. Slowly I scrambled to my feet. Then I ran my fingers over the inscription on that enormous horizontal slab of slate. As I began to read it my attention was immediately drawn to the names recorded there. It read as follows.

Sacred to the memory
of
HENRY WILLIAM BULLIVANT
1793 - 1849
And his wife
AGNES MARY BULLIVANT
1799 - 1861

The realisation suddenly hit me. I had been hiding from 'Mad Bull' Bullivant inside the table-top tomb of some of his ancestors!

That afternoon we each had our own story to tell of our escape from Brinton Copse. Rosie, Michael and Beth had made their way home quickly through the woods without mishap. Baz had spotted his dad's friend riding a bike through the middle of Brinton, so he had hitched a lift home on the crossbar. Georgie and Jimmy had taken the long route home along the road, while Charlie, the Professor and Robbie had fled into the woods. Unfortunately little Robbie arrived back soaking wet because, in trying to jump the stream, he had tripped and had fallen headlong into the middle of it. This time I was determined that I was not going to be the one to take him home to his mum! Finally I told my comrades how I had almost been caught by Scarface, and how I had been forced to hide inside the ancestral tomb of the Bullivant family.

Michael, Georgie, Rosie, Beth and I climbed up to the look-out and sat down. We needed to take stock of the situation.

"'Mad Bull' Bullivant is determined to get even with you, Tommy," Michael reminded me.

"The trouble is that he's always got those two ugly mates with him," remarked Georgie.

"That big one with the scar on his face bent down and looked inside the tomb where I was hiding," I told them. "I saw him really close up. He was horrible."

"That must have been really scary, Tommy," muttered Beth. "I think Tommy deserves another medal because I think he's ever so brave."

"Who are Ginger and Scarface anyway?" asked Rosie.

"We haven't got a clue who they are or where they've come from," admitted Michael. "They just seem to have appeared from nowhere in the last week or so."

Our conversation was disturbed rather abruptly by a shrill piping voice below us. Down below in the Jones's garden was Archie Fraser and he was talking to himself. He was scratching around in the soil, digging up worms and putting them into a jam jar. Then, as we watched, he wandered over to the fowl pen where Wilma and Cyril kept their hens. He opened the gate and started to throw the worms inside for the hens to eat. Having delivered all his worms to Wilma's feathered friends, Archie strolled away again to find some more. As he went about his digging, he babbled away to himself incessantly. Suddenly we noticed that the door of the fowl pen was still wide open, and all the hens, together with a magnificent large cockerel, were strutting around the garden. They seemed to be thoroughly enjoying themselves as they scratched and pecked about in the soil, searching for scraps of food.

When Archie looked around he also noticed that Wilma's hens had escaped.

"Grandma, grandma," he screamed, as he ran up the garden path.

Wilma appeared at the scullery door.

"Grandma, the hens have escaped and the gate to the hen house is wide open."

Soon Wilma and Cyril were hurrying down the garden path.

"I think those boys from next door must have been there, grandma," he said as they hurried beneath the apple tree. "I'm sure I saw them running away."

We looked at each other, scarcely able to believe our ears.

"Who did you see running away, Archie?" said Wilma, puffing and panting, her face red from rushing.

"Fat Georgie and his brother with the bad leg grandma; and that boy from Birmingham was with them as well, grandma."

"The horrible little liar," whispered Georgie. "I'm not fat, and we haven't been anywhere near her hens."

"He was the one who let them all escape," I murmured. "I saw him unfasten the gate to throw the worms inside."

We were then provided with some of the funniest entertainment we had ever seen. It was even better than some of the Laurel and Hardy films that we watched at the Palace cinema. We had great difficulty stifling our laughter as we watched Wilma, Cyril and Archie chasing several elusive hens and their impressive large cockerel round and round the garden, in order to drive them back into the pen. Poor Cyril, with his bad chest, had to keep stopping because he was having difficulty breathing. Every time he paused to catch his breath Wilma would start to rant and rave at him again. The more she chased about after the hens, the redder her scraggy face became. Her tight neat bun at the back of her head had come undone, and her long grey hair was now straggling out behind her as she huffed and puffed around the fruit bushes and between the rows of vegetables in pursuit of her poultry. Meanwhile Archie was careering all over the place, chasing after the poor birds like a starving fox, shrieking at the top of his voice and causing them to flutter and squawk in all directions.

Eventually Cyril was sent back to the cottage to fetch reinforcements in the form of Archie's mother and his older sister. When they arrived on the scene, their presence did nothing to inspire confidence that the problem was about to be resolved. Archie's mum was an extremely large lady who waddled down the path like an over-fed duck with chilblains. Her 17 year old daughter, Mavis, who was a scrawny-looking lass, hobbled along behind in a tight skirt and high-heeled shoes which were obviously crippling her feet. For half an hour we watched this pantomime unfold, as the entire Jones/Fraser family pursued their poultry among the raspberry canes, and between the rows of carrots and potatoes.

Finally when all the hens had been forced back into their pen, only the large reddish-brown cockerel with its fine curving display of tail feathers and bright red cockscomb was still at large. The five tired chasers managed to drive the majestic bird into a corner of the garden where it perched on top of a compost heap. We watched as Wilma crept forward to grab the magnificent bird. Realising that it about to be recaptured, the plucky cockerel made up its mind that it was not going to give in without a fight. Suddenly it flew at her feet first, with wings flapping and much squawking. As Wilma held her hands in front of her face and attempted to frighten the rebellious rooster away, the bird pecked at her viciously. Wilma thrashed her arms about to fend off the belligerent bird, causing a flurry of feathers to rise up into the air.

Archie now ran into the fray to assist his grandmother, but as soon as the fearless bird realised that Archie was getting involved, it turned its attention away from Wilma and launched itself at him instead. The determined cockerel flew straight at him and pecked him so hard that Archie let out a spine-chilling scream and fled back to the cottage in terror, with blood trickling down his cheek. The gallant rooster had defeated him and driven him from the field of battle. It then returned to top of the compost heap where it began to crow so loudly that the whole of Stretton and Brinton must have heard his triumphant call.

Every possible strategy was now used in an effort to persuade the reluctant creature to return to its pen. Mavis took off both her shoes and threw them at it, Cyril picked up a bean pole and prodded at it, and Archie's mum waddled about making clucking noises and flapping her arms in the hope that it would follow her, thinking she was an over-sized chicken. Meanwhile Wilma sat on an upturned bucket with her head in her hands, nursing her wounds. The final act of this comedy drew to a close when the cockerel finally decided to return to the pen of its own accord, attracted by a few handfuls of chicken feed which Cyril had thrown inside for the hens.

"That was so funny," laughed Georgie, as Cyril closed the fowl pen door and the family retired from the battlefield.

"Did you see the way that cockerel went for old Wilma?" I remarked.

"And it gave Archie a good pecking as well," chuckled Georgie.

"Perhaps we should persuade that cockerel to join our brigade so that it can sort out Bullivant, Scarface and Ginger," giggled Michael

I did not wish to be reminded of Bullivant, Scarface and Ginger. The most recent incident in the Brinton churchyard had scared the living daylights out of me, and I knew that I had been very lucky to escape. It seemed that wherever I went outside our village 'Mad Bull' Bullivant was there with those two hideous henchmen of his.

"I'm really scared of Scarface and Ginger," I admitted.

"You'll have to try to keep away from them," said the Professor.

"Yeah, but that's not going to be so easy," suggested Jimmy. "They always seem to be in Brinton and that's where our school is."

"Well, if we see them coming we'll have to run into school and tell Mr. Hardcastle," suggested Georgie.

That evening the members of the brigade met up in the HQ. Michael said that he had something very important to tell the brigade. The news which he delivered caused us great anxiety. He told us that in the next few days we would be facing the toughest test of our entire lives.

"I have heard that the German invasion is going to start in the next few days," he reported. "My dad was talking to PC Poynter, and he said that the police and Home Guard around here have been put on high alert because they have received information that some German soldiers are going to parachute into Stretton. They are coming here to blow up the main railway line and block Stretton tunnel so that trains can't get through. Our railway line is very important because it's a main line to London."

Everyone stared at the colonel open mouthed. This was it then! Hitler's invasion of Britain was about to begin.

"Everybody in the village will have to be ready, and the members of the Balaclava Brigade must do their bit," our colonel went on.

"But how are we going to stop German soldiers from blowing up the railway and capturing our village?" asked the Professor.

"They'll have real guns with them," said Jimmy nervously.

"And they'll shoot us all dead," said little Robbie, who was looking particularly worried.

"Yeah, we won't stand a chance against German soldiers with guns," agreed Georgie.

"Well, I ain't scared of no Jerry soldiers," muttered Baz. "I'm goin' to make meself another catapult and I'm goin' to 'shoot big stones at their 'eads."

Rosie had been very quiet until now. Finally she spoke up.

"There is something we can do," she informed everyone. "If they're going to blow up the railway line they'll have to go through Stretton Woods because the railway runs right through the middle of those woods."

"We could 'ide in them woods," said Baz, "and then we could jump out at 'em and fight 'em."

"But we'd all get killed," said the Professor.

"I ain't going to fight Hitler's soldiers in the woods and get killed," protested little Robbie.

"We don't have to fight them in the woods," insisted Rosie. "My dad always says, 'If the enemy is too strong, use guerrilla warfare. We may not be able to fight them in a battle, but we could use a guerrilla ambush to slow them down. That would give everybody in Stretton, especially the Home Guard, a bit more time."

"That's a great idea!" said Michael. "We don't want to come face to face with well-armed German soldiers, but we could arrange a guerrilla ambush in the woods! Then we shall all be heroes!"

Baz was looking extremely worried.

"Oooh! I ain't goin' in them woods," he said.

"What's the matter, Baz," I asked.

"I ain't goin' in them woods if there's gorillas in there," he muttered. "Gorillas is great big hairy monsters. They can pick you up and squeeze you to death."

"But there aren't any gorillas in Stretton Woods," the Professor assured him.

"*She* said there was gorillas in them woods," Baz insisted, pointing at Rosie.

"She didn't say anything about gorillas," explained the Professor. "Rosie said we'd have to use a guerrilla ambush. That means we would hide in the woods, set traps for the enemy and then quickly disappear through the trees again."

"So now you're sayin' there ain't no gorillas in our woods?" said Baz, who was becoming utterly confused. "Well I wish you'd stop talkin' about gorillas if there ain't none there, 'cus I don't like gorillas."

It was no good! We were never going to be able to persuade Baz that a guerrilla ambush did not involve huge hairy creatures. From now on we would refer to that kind of operation as a booby-trap ambush, so that poor Baz would not think we were fighting huge hairy gorillas. We knew that an ambush using booby-traps was our only chance of slowing down the German soldiers, but would we be able to come up with the right sort of plans for this kind of military operation?

Chapter 32

The Ambush in Stretton Woods

Michael was delighted with Rosie's suggestion.

"I think an ambush is just what we need!" exclaimed our colonel. "If we set some traps in the woods the German soldiers will fall right into them, and we won't even have to be there. We are going to organise one of the biggest and best military ambushes ever."

We all thought an ambush sounded like a great idea, and we began to think about what sort of traps we could set for those German invaders.

The Professor was the first person to come up with an idea.

"I've thought of a brilliant trap," he began. "In pre-historic times the cave people used to catch fierce wild animals by digging a big pit in the ground. Then they covered it over with thin branches and grass. When an animal came along it would tread right onto it and fall down inside."

"That's terrific," said Michael. "At the bottom of the pit we could put some spiky thorn branches, just like the ones we put in Bullivant's den in the summer holidays."

Everyone agreed that this sort of trap was just what we needed!

"I know what we could do," suggested Rosie. "We could get some long poles of wood, saw them halfway through in the middle and then put them across the stream like a bridge so that the cuts are underneath by the water. When the German soldiers run across our booby-trapped bridge the poles will break in the middle and they will tumble into the water."

"Yeah, and then they won't be able to fight," said Baz triumphantly.

"Their guns will probably be full of water," added Rosie.

Everyone thought that was a fantastic idea. I was now convinced that Rosie was a military genius.

I had thought of another way in which we could delay the German advance. I suggested that we could take some pieces of rope to the woods and tie each one between two trees so that it was stretched at ankle height in the long grass.

"Enemy soldiers rushing through the grass would be tripped up by the ropes and then they would fall over on top of one another," I suggested.

"With a bit of luck they might even accidentally fire their guns and shoot each other," suggested the Professor.

"We could prepare lots of traps like that in our woods if we could get enough rope," I said.

Everyone agreed that booby traps involving ropes stretched between trees in the long grass would be superb way of ambushing the invading Germans.

Now we knew that we had a superb master plan – the best ambush plan that any British army unit had ever come up with. By using ambush tactics we would be able to achieve a brilliant military victory without even coming into contact with our enemy. These were hit-and-run tactics at their very best! Those German troops were going to be in for quite a shock as they headed for that important railway line – thanks to the skill and military genius of the Balaclava Brigade!

"We'll have to set up our ambush pretty quickly," said Michael. "We'll go to the woods and do it first thing on Saturday morning."

"I can't wait," laughed Baz, who was getting very excited about our plans.

"I'd love to see what happens when Hitler's best soldiers fall right into our traps," giggled Charlie.

"They won't be in a fit state to blow anything up by the time we've finished with them," muttered Michael smugly.

When Saturday morning arrived the brigade assembled ready to go to the woods.

"Have we got everything we need?" Colonel Michael asked.

"We've got 4 spades, an axe, a saw, a chopper, some long pieces of rope and 6 long poles of timber," replied Sergeant Georgie, checking the items off in his head as he looked around our headquarters.

This was the day we had all been waiting for. We crossed Blore's Field, carrying the equipment over our shoulders. When we arrived in the woods Lance-Corporal Baz was ordered to climb the tallest tree, so that he could act as look-out in case anyone happened to come along while we were preparing our ambush. All morning we toiled away, digging a deep pit beside the path. This was not too difficult because the soil was very sandy. When the pit was deep enough we lined the bottom of it with twigs covered in sharp thorns, and then we covered it over with thin branches, pieces of turf and bracken. The whole area was then sprinkled with dead leaves from the trees to disguise the trap.

"How are we goin' to make sure they fall into it?" asked Private Robbie. "They're goin' to stick to the path, aren't they?"

"We haven't finished yet," said Colonel Michael. "We're going to block the path so that they will have to go across our pit."

An old tree stump and some branches were dragged into position to obstruct the path, and the pile of soil which we had dug from the pit was camouflaged with fallen leaves, twigs and small branches, giving it the appearance of a large bonfire ready for burning.

Next we set about sawing the timber poles half way through. These we placed across the stream so that the saw cuts were underneath and invisible from above. We constructed a couple of such bridges across the stream, and also prepared several trip ropes in the tall grass.

"Right chaps," said our colonel. "Everything's ready now. David is ready to defeat Goliath.!"

We had started to gather together all our tools and equipment when suddenly Lance-Corporal Baz scuttled down the tree from where he had been keeping watch.

"Them Jerries is comin'," he said excitedly. "I've just seen 'em and there's loads of 'em."

"How do you know it's the Germans," asked Colonel Michael.

" 'Cus I've seen 'em. I've seen their uniforms and their 'elmets. They've got guns with 'em. And they've got bits of twigs stuck all over them and dirt all over their faces."

"They'll be much dirtier than that by the time we've finished with them," giggled Corporal Charlie.

"They must have been dropped by parachute last night when it was dark," said Colonel Michael. "Listen! We'd better get away from here quickly. Follow me, chaps."

He turned and started to run, and we followed after him. After a while we stopped and stood silently in a group to listen. Now we could hear the enemy troops barging their way through thickets and trampling down the undergrowth. There was the snapping of twigs underfoot and the rustle of branches.

"They're getting closer," said our colonel.

My nerves were starting to tingle and I was now beginning to shake all over.

Suddenly I heard a loud crack and a splintering of timber, followed by a couple of high-pitched strangled cries. There followed several loud splashes accompanied by desperate yells of "Aaaaagh!", "Ooooh!" and "Eeeeee!"

"Some of them have tumbled into the stream," giggled Sergeant Georgie.

More piercing shrieks and yells followed, suggesting that our concealed pit, lined with prickly thorn branches, had also claimed several victims.

But still some of the troops were charging forward. Suddenly more loud cries of despair filled the air, and I could imagine ugly helmeted German paratroopers tumbling over our trip ropes and crashing down on top of one another in a huge untidy heap.

"Right!" whispered Colonel Michael. "Our ambush has worked. Now, listen carefully! We'll make a dash for our HQ, and then we'll decide what to do next. Come on, chaps! Let's get going!"

We ran like the wind. Along the path between the trees we raced until we came to the edge of the woods. Over the stile we leapt and soon we were sprinting across Blore's field without as much as a glance over our shoulders.

When at last we arrived back at our headquarters, everyone flopped down onto our straw-filled seats. We were totally exhausted but very happy.

"That ambush was brilliant," panted Michael.

"Yeah," gasped Charlie, "I heard some of them splash head first into the stream."

"Did you hear them screaming when they fell into that big hole on top of those thorns," yelled Jimmy.

"I'm sure lots of them tripped over our ropes," I said.

"Our ambush in Stretton Woods has been a brilliant victory!" enthused Michael.

"Yes," I agreed. "Today I think the Balaclava Brigade has covered itself in glory."

"Yeah and we've just covered Hitler's blokes in loads of dirt and mucky water," laughed Charlie.

"You lot wait here," ordered our colonel. "I'm going to tell somebody that the German soldiers are in our woods."

Before Michael had chance to leave Beth spoke up.

"I wonder where Rosie is. She hasn't come back yet."

"You don't think the Germans have captured her, do you?" I asked anxiously.

I heard footsteps outside, the gate of our HQ was flung open and Rosie entered looking red-faced and breathless.

"Where did you get to?" asked Charlie. "You're not going to tell us you got lost in the woods!"

Rosie stared at us.

"My dad always says that it's very important for an army to find out how successful their mission has been, so I stayed behind to see."

"You could have been captured and taken prisoner," I gasped.

"Or even shot dead," stammered little Robbie.

"Yes," agreed Michael, as he stood by the open gate. "I gave the order for everybody to escape immediately. You disobeyed my order. Why did you stay behind? We all know that our ambush was a brilliant success."

"I don't think it was that much of a success!" muttered Rosie.

"Not a success!" yelled Michael angrily. "What are you talking about? It was a fantastic success."

"What was wrong with it then?" I asked.

Rosie's eyes flitted anxiously from face to face before continuing.

"Well, after you lot had all run away I waited and listened. I could hear people shouting instructions to each other. I knew something wasn't quite right, so I decided to climb a tree to have a better look. Through my binoculars I watched the soldiers crawling up the bank of the stream and climbing out of the pit. I could see that they were all soaking wet and covered in mud. Some of them were pulling their rifles up the bank out of the water."

"But that's just what we planned, isn't it?" said the Professor.

"I bet those German soldiers weren't defeated like that when they invaded some of those other countries," laughed Charlie.

"They've never come across anybody like the Balaclava Brigade before, have they?" said the Professor proudly.

"Yeah, we dain't 'alf show 'em!" yelled Baz gleefully.

Georgie agreed.

"I think we've just taught Hitler's lot a lesson they'll never forget," he said with immense pride.

I glanced at Rosie. She was not joining in with our expressions of delight, and there was a rather anxious troubled look on her face. Then she spoke up again.

"When I looked through my binoculars from the top of the tree I could see that the soldiers we'd ambushed weren't Germans. Those chaps were all shouting to each other in English. Do you realise what we've done? We've just ambushed the Stretton and Brinton Home Guard by mistake!"

Chapter 33

The Brigade HQ is Invaded Again

The next morning when we went down for breakfast Mrs. Millward was standing at the table cutting slices of bread on her wooden bread board. She went across to a large black frying pan on the hob beside the fire and placed one thick slice into it. The bread sizzled noisily as soon as it came into contact with the fat.

"Cor! Great! It's our Sunday morning fried breakfast!" I thought as I sat down at the table.

The latch on the door to the yard rattled and Georgie's dad entered the room.

"What were you lot doing yesterday?" he asked, staring straight at Jimmy, Georgie and me.

We glanced at each other uncomfortably.

"Oh, we were just playing," Georgie replied.

"You didn't see that kid from Brinton by any chance, did you?"

"What kid's that, dad?" asked Jimmy, assuming the angelic look of a cathedral choirboy.

"That Bullivant kid!"

"No we didn't see him at all yesterday," answered Georgie truthfully.

"Well, I've just been talkin' to old Mr. Jenks in the street. Yesterday afternoon, he went with the all the other Home Guard blokes to the woods. They were doin' some trainin' ready for when the Germans land. They'd covered themselves all over with bits of branches and twigs. When they were runnin' through the woods they fell into some traps that somebody had set for them. They're sure it was that kid, Bullivant, and his mates from Brinton."

We all tried to look extremely surprised and suitably shocked.

"Old Mr. Jenks was tellin' me that they'd dug a great big hole in the ground and covered it over. 'He fell right into it on top of a load of thorns. Three other chaps fell right on top of him, and they couldn't get out. When Mr. Jenks did get out he was covered all over from head to toe in dirt and mud, and he'd got heaps of thorns stuck in his backside."

"What else did they do?" inquired Jimmy, still adopting an air of wide-eyed innocence.

"They sent several of the chaps tumblin' into the stream. When poor old Mr. Fredericks got out he was soaked to the skin, and now his pocket watch won't work. They tripped up some of the other chaps with ropes in the long grass, so that they all fell on top of each other in a great heap. Mr. Stubbs said three of his mates fell on top of him. They hurt 'is chest but, worse than that, they crushed his brand new packet of 20 Capstan fags that were in his top pocket. That Bullivant kid is a real bad lot. If he belonged to me I'd give him a right good thrashin'."

I glanced sideways at Georgie. He was staring down at the tablecloth. Mrs. Millward stepped forward and put our fried breakfasts on the table in front of us.

"I saw that Bullivant lad with two older chaps the other day," she said. "Nasty-looking lot they were. I don't know who his friends were. I've never seen them before. Do you know, that Bullivant lad's got a voice like one of those *grannyphone* records! It goes on and on without ever stopping."

Georgie coughed nervously but resisted the temptation to inform his mum that she must have meant 'gramophone records' rather than *grannyphone* records. Jimmy was fumbling about with something in his pocket and I was gazing blankly into space.

"Come on, you boys!" said Georgie's mum, who was standing with her hands on her hips, staring at us. "What's the matter with you three this morning? Your breakfasts will go cold if you don't get a move on!"

We cleared our plates quickly and hurried down to our headquarters. Michael, Beth, Rosie, Charlie, Baz and the Professor were already sitting inside talking about our failed mission of the day before.

"We're in big trouble now," said Michael.

"It's not our fault," protested Charlie, "if the stupid Home Guard blokes are daft enough to walk straight into our ambush."

"I reckon they're bound to tell PC Poynter what's happened," said Michael. "Before we know it, he'll be coming round to all our houses, and when he does my dad will go barmy."

"I hope he doesn't come round to our house," said Rosie. "I don't know what I would say to Mr. and Mrs. Fredericks because they are really good to me."

"It's OK. Don't worry," interrupted Georgie. "They don't know it was us. They think it was Bullivant and his mates that ambushed them."

"How do you know that?" inquired Michael.

" 'Cus our dad was talking to Grandpa Jenks this morning," Georgie answered, "and old Jenks told him that it was Bullivant's lot that attacked them."

"It was all your fault, Baz," cried Charlie.

"What were my fault?" shouted Baz.

"It was your fault that we ambushed the Home Guard by mistake," Charlie replied.

"It weren't my fault!" Baz yelled.

"Well, you were the one who was acting as look-out," answered Charlie. "You should have told us that it was the Home Guard coming instead of a load of Hitler's soldiers."

"Well, it weren't my fault," repeated Baz. "I could 'ardly see 'em from up in that tree. They was all covered with branches and leaves and stuff."

"Charlie! You can't blame Baz," I said.

"No! You wouldn't have done any better," yelled the Professor, looking sideways at his twin brother.

"You couldn't have even climbed up that tree in the first place."

"It's a good job I stayed behind, isn't it?" said Rosie. "We would be in loads of trouble if Michael had told PC Poynter that the Germans were in Stretton woods."

Michael said nothing. He was very reluctant to admit it, but by disobeying his order and staying behind, Rosie had saved him from having to answer some very difficult questions from our local bobby. Everyone thought this must be our lucky day, for it seemed as though we had got away with it this time. We were feeling rather smug that Bullivant was going to get the blame for something that we had done.

"I'm going to celebrate by having one of our apples," said Jimmy. "Anybody else want one?"

"I'd like a nice red one, please," said Beth.

"And me," answered Charlie.

"And me," said Rosie.

"I'll 'ave one of them big sour cookers," shouted Baz, as Jimmy disappeared into the pig-house.

"Bring him the smallest one," said Charlie. "We don't want him being sick in our headquarters."

Suddenly from behind the black-out curtain there arose a loud cry.

"Where are they?" Jimmy yelled. "Our apples have all gone!"

Chapter 34

A Plan is Hatched for Archie

Everybody leapt to their feet and dashed into the pig-house to join Jimmy. He was right! The apple boxes were empty and the wrapping papers were strewn all over the floor.

"Where 'ave they gone to?" asked Baz.

"Well, they haven't put their hats and coats on and walked out of here, have they?" shouted Charlie.

"It's that Archie Fraser!" muttered Michael between clenched teeth. "He's been inside our headquarters."

"The thieving little rat!" exclaimed Jimmy.

"Somehow we've got to stop him!" muttered the Professor.

"Yes, we'll have to think up a brilliant way of sorting out Archie Fraser," I murmured.

"Yeah, I agree with Tommy," said Michael. "We need to find a way of scaring the pants off him."

"What do you think Archie's most frightened of?" asked Rosie.

"I know what he's frightened of," said Beth who was in his class at school. "He's scared of the dark, and he's frightened of ghosts. He's always writing about it in his stories."

"That's it then!" said Rosie, crashing her hand onto the table. "That's what we'll do! We'll scare him with stories of ghosts in the dark."

Once again it seemed that Rosie had come up with the perfect solution!

Instantly the brigade set about devising a plan whereby Archie would be convinced that Wilma's place was haunted.

"First we need to spread a story about a ghost that haunts Archie's garden about the middle of October," Rosie suggested.

"We could say that a murderer once lived in our village," continued the Professor, "and that he killed a little lad in Wilma's garden because he kept pinching things."

"Yeah, p'rhaps 'e kept pinchin' all that bloke's money," added Baz.

We could not believe our ears! Baz had actually contributed something to a story. That must be a first!

"We could say that he killed the little lad when he was going to the privy late at night in the dark," suggested Michael.

"And we could spread it round that he only appears in October which is when he killed the little lad," added the Professor.

"Yes, every October he wanders around after dark, looking for little lads to murder and trying to get into the cottage through the bedroom windows," said Rosie

Both Michael and Rosie had very vivid imaginations, and I was almost beginning to think that I might have heard this killer ghost prowling around the place when I had lived there.

"So all we've got to do now is to spread this story around in the playground so that all the kids at school start talking about it," stressed Rosie. "Jimmy, Baz and Beth – you would be the best ones to do that because you're in his class. If everybody in your class starts talking to him about this ghost then Archie will begin to think it's true."

"We could back it up with a few ghostly sounds and scary noises in the evenings," suggested the Professor.

"Even better than that," said Michael, "we could arrange for that ghost to suddenly appear in Wilma's garden after dark just as Archie's going to the privy."

"But Charlie reckons there ain't no such things as ghosts," protested Baz.

"He doesn't mean a real ghost, Baz," said Georgie giggling. "He means somebody dressed up, pretending to be a ghost."

"I could dress up as a ghost," said Baz. "I'm a hexpert at dressin' up."

"We also need somebody who can make really good ghost noises," said Rosie.

Since both Michael and I admitted that we could not make convincing ghost noises we said that we would act as judges while the others demonstrated their skills.

"I'm a hexpert at ghost noises," said Baz.

"Go on then, lets hear you," said Georgie.

Baz stood up, threw his head back and let out a deafening shrill note.

"That's no good," said Michael. "That sounds nothing like a ghost."

"Sounds more like old Grandma Jenks when she sang *Away in a Manger* at last year's carol service in the Baptist Chapel," laughed Charlie.

Georgie's ghost sound was not much better. It was a much deeper yowling sound similar to the noise made by Mrs. Clamp's aggressive tom cat when he's on the prowl in the middle of the night looking for a fight. The Professor's attempt was even worse. It was far too soft and gentle like a pair of love-sick doves cooing to each across the

Stretton roof tops. Charlie had a go next. He threw back his head, opened his mouth really wide and let out a deafening howl which sounded more like the cry of a wild dog in a one of those cowboy films which we sometimes saw at the pictures. Finally when Jimmy tried, a feeble little noise came out of his mouth like that of a croaking bull frog in distress.

Michael and I had not heard anything yet that sounded remotely like a ghost calling. Beth and Robbie were ruled out since they were not allowed to stay out when it was getting dark, and so this was turning out to be a disaster. Until now Rosie had remained very quiet.

"I suppose I'd better have a go then," she said with a smile.

She put her cupped hands to her mouth and began to send forth the most realistic ghostly night call we had ever heard. "Ooooooooooh!" There was brief pause and then she called again, "Ooooooooooh!" The sound began softly, built up to a spine-tingling climax and then tailed off again very gently. It was absolutely terrific. It sounded so ghost-like that the hairs on our necks started to stand on end, and we were all beginning to feel little shivers running down the middle of our backs. The contest was well and truly over! Rosie was the one who was going to perform the night call of the dreaded Stretton killer ghost.

It was now felt that we were ready to teach Archie a lesson. Over the next few days our carefully created story was spread around at school. Jimmy and Beth both wrote ghost stories in class about the haunted cottage garden in Stretton where Archie Fraser lived, and where a murderer's ghost still haunted the place, looking for little sneak thieves to kill. Baz didn't write a story as usual, but he drew a picture of the Stretton ghost strangling a little lad as he walked down the garden path to the privy.

Children in the playground began to talk about Archie's cottage.

"I wouldn't like live in your cottage," I heard a little girl telling Archie. "There's a horrible ghost that wanders around in your garden."

"Yeah, he goes round making noises and looking for little boys who pinch things and then he kills them," said a small lad with great relish.

"You'd better watch out 'cus sometimes he gets into the cottage through the bedroom windows," said another.

"That ghost of yours starts his haunting in the middle of October," another boy told him. "He'll be starting soon. I wouldn't like to live in your cottage."

At first Archie scoffed at these claims, and laughed at the people who made them. But the more he heard about this ghost the more anxious he started to become. He began to keep himself to himself. He became fidgety and nervous. But his problems really started when the next part of our plan was put into operation!

Chapter 35

A Ghost on the Prowl

A few nights later when it was dark we all gathered beneath Archie Fraser's bedroom window and waited until the blackout curtains were drawn across. When we felt sure that Archie was alone, Michael picked up a long clothes prop with a bunch of twigs tied to one end of it. Slowly and deliberately he began to scrape the twigs over the outside of the window pane and Rosie, with her hands cupped to her mouth, let out a long loud nocturnal ghost call, "Oooooooooooooh!" How would Archie react? We did not have to wait long to find out. We heard a loud piercing scream from inside his bedroom, followed by a high-pitched little voice yelling, "Grandma! Grandma! There's a ghost trying to get in through my window." This outburst was followed by the sound of a door slamming shut. After that everything went quiet. We looked at each other and nodded. That would do for a start!

The next night we changed our tactics. A bright full moon hung high in the night sky, illuminating the garden with a subdued silver light. The only sound we could hear was the gentle rustling of the leaves on the bushes and the apple tree. Michael, Rosie, Georgie, Jimmy, Charlie, the Professor, Baz and I were lying in wait, concealed behind the wall of our headquarters. We heard the scullery door open, and then the sound of Archie's footsteps running down the garden path. We watched as he tugged open the privy door and disappeared inside. We heard him slide the huge iron bolt across. At this point Michael nudged Rosie, and our expert ghost impersonator cupped her hands around her mouth. A long low spine-tingling call floated out onto the night air. "Ooooooooooooh!"

Instantly there was a shrill scream from inside the privy, followed by some loud howling.

"Grandma! Grandma!" the wailing lad yelled.

I could hear Archie's heels thumping against the front of the pine box upon which he was sitting as he thrashed his legs about in blind panic. After a while the kicking subsided, and we heard the giant bolt on the privy door slide back again. The door opened slightly, and one terrified eye squinted out. At that moment Rosie uttered another long burst of her phantom call. "Ooooooooooooh!" Immediately the privy door was flung wide open, and a small blubbering hunched figure burst out, clutching the waist band of his unfastened trousers in front of him. He tore up the garden path like greased lightning, yelling at the top of his voice, "Grandma! Grandma! It's that ghost! He's after me again!"

"Your ghost calls were fantastic, Rosie," I whispered.

"They made me feel a bit funny," muttered Georgie.

"Did you see the look in his eye when he peeped out of that door?" murmured the Professor.

"I reckon that really scared him," laughed Michael.

"He was so frightened he didn't even have time to fasten his trousers," giggled Charlie.

"We haven't finished with him yet," sniggered Michael. "In fact we've only just started."

The following evening our brigade decided to put the third part of the plan into operation. The night was particularly still and quiet. There was no breeze and the moon was obscured by a bank of cloud high in the sky. Once again we lay in wait beside the wall of our HQ. Soon we heard Wilma's scullery door open, and two voices were talking.

"Don't be so silly, Archie!"

"You come down the garden with me, Grandma."

"You'll be alright, Archie. There isn't a ghost in the garden."

The door closed again. We saw the shadowy figure of Archie, creeping anxiously down the garden path. He pushed open the privy door, disappeared inside and the heavy bolt rattled across. After Archie had been in there for quite a long time, we heard the bolt slide back again. Very slowly the door opened and Archie peeped out nervously. Then very slowly the door opened wide and Archie emerged.

At that very moment the moon peeped out from behind the bank of cloud, and a tall ghostly figure clad in white emerged from behind the wall of the pigsty, and began to glide up the garden path towards the privy door. As Archie turned round, the pale moonlight cast a mysterious light upon this strange apparition, and an elongated spine-chilling supernatural cry disturbed the silence. "Oooooooooooooooooh!" Poor Archie leapt high in the air, uttered a shrill squeal and fled up the path towards the cottage like a terrified fox with a pack of vicious hounds on its tail. By the time he reached the cottage door he was shrieking hysterically.

"Grandma! Grandma! Let me in! He's after me again!"

We crept into our headquarters and switched on our torch. Michael took off the enormous white tablecloth which had been covering him, and threw it onto the floor.

"I knew me tablecloth from the jumble sale would come in 'andy," whispered Baz.

"Did you see the way he ran," laughed the Professor.

"He was really scared that time," giggled Jimmy.

"I reckon it's a good job he'd just been to the toilet," chuckled Charlie.

"How long are we going to keep doing this?" I asked.

Although I accepted that Archie was a despicable little reptile, I was beginning to feel quite sorry for him. I recollected how terrified I had been when I had visited that privy late at night before going to bed. When I had lived in Wilma's cottage I, too, had been frightened of the dark shadows and the wind in the trees and the bushes. But I had never been faced with realistic ghost noises, and phantoms clad in white gliding up the garden path.

"We'll carry on for as long as it takes," replied Michael. "Tomorrow night we'll go back to scraping those twigs over his bedroom window again."

"Don't you think we should give it a rest for a night or two," I suggested.

"I'd like to climb up to 'is bedroom window with something 'orrible all over me face to frighten 'im when 'e shuts 'is bedroom curtains," said Baz.

"You wouldn't need anything covering *your* face to frighten him," chortled Charlie.

Despite my reservations, all the other members of the brigade were convinced that we should continue with our plan until it was clear that Archie had been well and truly beaten into submission.

Chapter 36

The Champions

The next morning when we boarded the bus for school Archie was not there. We thought he had probably been too frightened to get to sleep the previous night, and therefore had been allowed to catch up on his sleep that morning. When Georgie and I collected the registers to take them to Mr. Hardcastle we could hear voices in the corridor. As we turned the corner near Mr. Hardcastle's room Archie's mum was talking to our headmaster.

"Crikey! What's she here for?" whispered Georgie.

We stopped and waited a short distance away.

"You don't think she's going to complain about us, do you?" I murmured.

"Some bigger boys from our village keep being horrible to my Archie," began Mrs. Fraser, "and he's only been here a short time."

"Oh, I'm very sorry to hear that," replied the head. "Can you tell me who these boys are?"

"It happens all the time in Stretton. There are some terrible kids in that village, you know. They're making poor Archie's life a misery, and he doesn't deserve it. He's such a good little lad."

"What sort of things are they doing to him, Mrs. Fraser?"

"It all started when one of them accused our Archie of pinching his toy aeroplane. I knew my Archie hadn't taken it. Do you know, that little lad had broken his plane himself, and then he'd had thrown it into the garden because he thought he was going to get into trouble with his mum?"

"I will certainly speak to these boys from Stretton," interrupted Mr. Hardcastle.

"Archie says they keep hitting him and calling him names, just because he comes from London. One day they threw stones at him and made him fall out of an apple tree. He really hurt himself, poor little lad. They're terrible, those Stretton kids. Do you know, the other day they let my mother's hens out of the fowl pen? Archie watched them do it. It took my mother, my father, my daughter, Archie and me nearly half an hour to get all those hens back inside their pen."

"Well, Mrs. Fraser, if you will let me know who these boys are, I will certainly have a word with them and put a stop to it," Mr. Hardcastle assured her.

"Things have got so bad now that our Archie has become quite ill? These kids are affecting him so much that he keeps imagining that there's a ghost in the garden. And he reckons he can hear it trying to get into his bedroom through the window. Then last night, when he went to the toilet, he thought he saw this white ghost walking up the garden path. He was in a terrible state when he got back in the house. My mother even went outside to have a look around but, of course, there was nothing there."

"I will certainly look into it for you, Mrs. Fraser!"

"Well, that won't be necessary now. You see, we're not going to be living in Stretton any longer. I'm taking him right away from those dreadful kids. We're going up to Scotland to live with his dad's parents. I've come to tell you that we shall be leaving on Saturday."

Having delivered her complaint and her message, she turned and waddled off down the corridor like a duck heading for water. Georgie and I stepped forward and handed the registers to Mr. Hardcastle.

"You two lads live in Stretton, don't you?" he said, staring down at us.

"Yes, Mr. Hardcastle," we replied with one voice.

"Do you know of any boys who have been ill-treating young Archie Fraser?"

"No, Mr. Hardcastle," we replied together.

"We don't have anything to do with Archie Fraser when we're out playing," Georgie assured him.

Mr. Hardcastle gave us a long hard look before turning and walking into his room.

At dinnertime the members of the Balaclava Brigade (apart from Michael who was at Oakthorpe Senior School) were kicking a ball around in the playground when an overweight, cumbersome Brinton lad, who normally moved around at the pace of a sick snail, came up and challenged us to a football match in the school yard at the end of the afternoon.

"Our team, the Brinton Bullets, will stick your Stretton lot at footie after school," he said. "And whoever wins will be 'The Champions.'"

"But we have to catch the bus home," said Beth.

"That don't matter!" shouted Baz, who was always up for a challenge, "We can walk 'ome through the woods."

"Yeah, we'll stick you!" cried Charlie.

"And we'll wallop you," yelled Jimmy.

Having arranged the match, the large lad, who claimed to be the captain of the Brinton Bullets, crawled away at the speed of an injured tortoise.

"What are we going to call our team," asked Robbie.

"The Stretton Sharpshooters would be a good name," suggested the Professor.

"Yeah," said Charlie, "then it would be Brinton versus Stretton."

And so it was agreed that after school the Stretton Sharpshooters would play the Brinton Bullets in a football final to determine which team could call themselves 'The Champions'.

That evening after school we went into the playground to prepare for the match. Two gas mask boxes were placed at each end of the yard for the goals. It was Robbie's little rubber ball that we would be playing with, and so our team went out to practise as soon as lessons were over. Baz and Rosie were rehearsing their shooting at goal while Beth was supposed to be practising catching the ball. Unfortunately she insisted on ducking and hiding her face whenever a shot flew near her. Every time Robbie attempted to kick the ball he missed it completely as usual, of course.

When the Brinton Bullets came out led by their large sloth-like captain, they looked a comical bunch. There was a skinny little lad with straggly hair, legs like a sparrow and long shorts which came down to his knobbly knee caps; a solemn-faced little boy with a mop of straw-coloured curls; a very plump girl with wide eyes, large dimples and one long plaited pigtail - she was almost as round as the ball we were going to be playing with; a thick-set little chap with rosy cheeks and legs like tree stumps; a dreamy-looking young fellow with small round glasses, a pair of grey short trousers much too big for him and a bright blue jumper far too small for him; a grubby-looking boy with a tattered sleeveless pullover and muddy Wellington boots; and a small elfin-like little girl who looked as if she would have the utmost difficulty withstanding anything stronger than a gentle breeze.

"We'll beat this lot easy," jeered Baz, as he watched the opposition troop out onto the pitch. The stocky little lad was busy exercising his tree-trunk legs; 'Sparrow Legs' was sprinting up and down the length of the pitch, while the little lad in Wellingtons was fishing sludge-covered marbles out of a nearby school drain.

During the opening minute of the game, there was a bitter dispute. The serious-looking lad with straw-coloured hair, who appeared to be their only good player, had been preparing to shoot at our goal with only Beth to beat. Suddenly Robbie came in from the side and took a mighty kick at the ball. Once again his aim was not up to scratch. The would-be goal scorer screamed out in pain and hopped three times round the playground clutching his right ankle.

"Foul! Penalty!" the Brinton players all shouted.

"That weren't no penalty," yelled Baz. "That were a haccident."

The Brinton team gathered around our goal, protesting that it was clearly a penalty. A furious argument ensued with certain members of both teams shouting at the tops of their voices. Baz even resorted to a little ungentlemanly pushing and shoving. This heated dispute was finally resolved when the Brinton captain finally accepted that it was definitely an accident rather than a penalty. He took the members of his team on one side to inform them that there was absolutely no doubt about it. That kick on the ankle had not been intentional, and therefore could not be considered a foul. He had been persuaded to change his mind when young Robbie said he would pick up his ball and take it home if anyone else said that his tackle was a foul.

A host of other disasters followed for the Brinton team. Quite by accident Georgie cannoned into the lad with sparrow legs, sending him crashing into the wall of the air-raid shelter. This unfortunate accident caused the fragile-looking lad to hobble around for a while, wincing and groaning every time he put his left foot onto the ground, until eventually he picked up his jumper and gas mask and hobbled off home. The sloth-like captain delivered a mighty full-blooded kick at the ball but accidentally hit the churchyard wall by mistake. He spent the rest of the game sitting down on the school step, minus his shoe and sock, clutching his injured toes. Whilst running at full speed, the plump little girl unwittingly trod on the ball, fell down and then rolled over and over several times, before crashing into the air-raid shelter wall. She subsequently decided that football was a ruffian's game, and she hobbled away home. Immediately afterwards without meaning to do so, Robbie's hobnailed boot trod rather heavily on the toe of the grubby little lad's Wellington, causing him to hop off the pitch and go back to exploring the mysteries the school drain. A few minutes later, the dreamy lad with the glasses and the ill-fitting clothes was gazing up into the sky, staring at a large flock of geese flying overhead, when a thunderous shot from Rosie smacked him on the side of the head, laying him flat on his back for several seconds. When he eventually came to his senses he remembered that he had to go home early, so he promptly left.

In the meantime the ball was permanently at the Brinton end of the pitch, for Baz and Rosie were scoring goals at will. One by one the Brinton players had hobbled off and limped away home like the remnants of Napoleon's army fleeing the battlefield after Waterloo. All opposition finally evaporated when their goalie, the only Brinton player left on the pitch, said that he was starving and was going home to have his tea. With no Brinton players remaining, Baz and Rosie scored another 15 goals between them before we decided that there was little point in playing on without any opposition. The Professor, who had been keeping the score, announced that the Stretton Sharpshooters had won the match by 36 goals to nil, and all our goals had been scored by Baz and Rosie, our amazing pair of sharpshooters.

"We thrashed 'em!" shouted Baz, as we walked through the school gates and headed for the woods and the path home.

When we stepped onto the pavement outside school I glanced up the road. Walking towards us were three shambling figures. It was 'Mad Bull' Bullivant and his two older mates.

"Oh heck!" I shouted. "It's 'Mad Bull'! Quick! Run!"

We turned tail and fled back into school, hoping that Mr. Hardcastle would still be there. We felt sure he would sort out those bullies. But what was Baz doing? He had started to run in the opposite direction. Baz had caught sight of a bike leaning up against the garden wall of an ivy-covered cottage. Surely he was not going to take that bike and ride away on it in order to escape. I soon realised that was exactly what he intended to do!

When Baz reached the bike, he pulled it away from the wall and prepared to leap onto the saddle. Before he could do so the ginger-headed fellow grabbed him by the jumper. He wrenched the bike away from Baz, picked it up with one hand and hurled it into the middle of the road with a resounding crash. The bell fell from the handlebars and went clattering across the road onto the grass verge. Baz was kicking and struggling to get free but it was no good. Bullivant's ginger mate was far too strong for him.

"Quick get 'is bike," yelled Bullivant

Scarface stepped forward, picked up the bike and began to inspect it.

"It's a rubbish bike, is this one," he shouted, and he hurled it down onto the road again with tremendous force. There was a terrible clatter of metal on tarmac and the sound of breaking glass.

The bike's front lamp, together with its black-out hood, had fallen off and was skidding across the road, leaving a trail of broken glass behind.

"I'll 'ave this bike," shouted Bullivant.

"It ain't got a bell or a lamp now," shouted Scarface with a twisted grin.

"That don't matter," yelled Bullivant. "It's in better nick than mine."

Bullivant stooped and picked up the bike. Then he began to ride it round and round in the middle of the road.

"This bike's alright," shouted Bullivant to his friends, who were each holding Baz by the arms. Our little lance-corporal was struggling violently and yelling at the top of his voice.

"Let go of me! Get off me!"

"This is the kid what was calling us names in the woods," Ginger shouted to Bullivant.

"Yeah, 'e needs to learn some manners, 'e does," cried Scarface.

"Get off! Leave me alone!" Baz was screaming.

We could do nothing to help our comrade. We could only watch in horror as the brave little lad was being dragged away, struggling and screaming.

"Poor old Baz," muttered Charlie. "I wouldn't like to be in his boots right now."

Chapter 37

Another Order of St. George

"Look at the way Baz is wriggling to get free," whispered Georgie.

"He's being really brave," said Beth who was full of admiration.

"I reckon we ought to give him another Balaclava medal," suggested the Professor.

"If we ever see him again," muttered Jimmy.

"Well, we can still give him another medal," said the Professor.

"I can't understand why he didn't follow us back into school," muttered Rosie.

We were hiding in the playground, peering over the school wall. We could see Bullivant riding his newly acquired bicycle round and round in the middle of the road, while Scarface and the Ginger were struggling to keep hold of Baz, who looked as slippery as an eel that had just come out of the river.

It was then that we heard a booming voice.

"Oy! You! Get off that bike!"

Coming out of the ivy-covered cottage was a tall figure, dressed in a flowing black cape and black domed helmet. It was PC Poynter. As soon as Scarface and Ginger spotted our local bobby, they threw down their sticks, dropped Baz as if he were a heavy sack of coal, and dashed away up the road as fast as they could run. Bullivant stopped his bike in the middle of the road, put one foot onto the ground and turned round to see who was shouting. When he saw the local policeman racing towards him, he stood up on the pedals and attempted to ride away.

"Stop him, Baz," shouted Rosie.

Baz was still scrambling to his feet, but as 'Mad Bull' Bullivant rode past him, our brave little lance-corporal picked up the stick which Scarface had thrown down and jabbed it at Bullivant. I saw the end of the stick jam between the spokes of Bullivant's front wheel. The bicycle stopped dead in its tracks, before standing vertically on its front tyre. Instantly Bullivant somersaulted head first over the handlebars, landing in a sprawling heap on his back in the middle of the road with the damaged bicycle on top of him. Almost immediately PC Poynter was there to grab him by the collar. The rest of us dashed out of the playground, and raced up the road to see what was going to happen next. We saw the policeman drag Bullivant to his feet, and then he glanced down at his bicycle. The cycle lamp was lying in bits in the middle of the road, the bell was missing from the handlebars, the black leather saddle was badly damaged and the front wheel was a complete wreck with several spokes sticking out at right angles.

"Theft of a bicycle!" bawled PC Poynter in Bullivant's ear.

"But 'e said it were 'is bike," protested the cowardly bully, pointing at Baz. " 'E said I could 'ave a go on it."

"No I never!" replied Baz. " 'E just pinched it."

"Theft of a bicycle! Criminal damage! I'm going to throw the book at you, sonny," the policeman bellowed, staring directly into Bullivant's face at close range.

"I've had dealings with you before," PC Poynter snarled as he dragged his captive around so that his face was clearly visible. "Your name's William Bullivant, if I'm not mistaken?"

We did not need a closer look.

"Yes," we all shouted.

"He goes to Oakthorpe Senior School," cried Georgie.

"He lives in Jubilee Terrace, Brinton," the Professor yelled.

"Yeah, Number 4," shouted Charlie.

Bullivant grimaced and curled his lip.

The policeman picked up his bicycle with one hand, and still clasping Bullivant firmly by the scruff of the neck with the other, he set off up the road towards No. 4 Jubilee Terrace, wheeling his damaged bike by his side.

"I think Baz acted like a hero," I said.

"He did brilliantly to stop Bullivant from escaping," agreed Rosie.

"Yeah, it's thanks to Baz that PC Poynter managed to cop hold of him," added Jimmy.

"I think Baz was ever so brave," said Beth.

"Those two big blokes had a job to keep hold of him," said Robbie with a mighty sniff.

Baz was delighted with such gushing praise from his comrades.

"Are you gonna tell our colonel about what I've done?" asked Baz.

"I shall do more than that, Baz," I replied. "I'm going to recommend you for another Balaclava Brigade medal."

During the journey home Baz would not stop talking. He wanted to know what sort of a medal I would be suggesting he should have. Then he wondered if Colonel Michael would promote him to a rank higher than lance-corporal. He said he wanted to be the brigade's special commando or secret operations 'hexpert'.

That evening the brigade congregated inside our headquarters. We had a great deal to tell our colonel. Georgie and I told him that we had overheard Mrs. Fraser telling Mr. Hardcastle that her family was leaving Stretton for good on Saturday, and that they were going to live in Scotland.

"I can't wait to see the back of Archie Fraser," said Beth.

"We shall all be glad to see him leave our village," I agreed.

I was now beginning to think of myself as one of the Stretton lads even though Bullivant always referred to me as 'that Brummie kid'.

We also told our colonel the whole story of how Baz had tied to wriggle free from Scarface and Ginger, and how he had finally managed to prevent Bullivant from escaping on PC Poynter's bike. We emphasised that, because of Baz's brave actions, Bullivant had been apprehended by our local policeman. Everybody agreed that Baz had been extremely courageous.

"I think that we should award Lance-Corporal Baz our highest award, the Order of St. George for Valour," I proposed.

There were unanimous shouts of approval from everyone apart from Michael.

"I don't know about that," protested our colonel. "The Order of St. George for Valour is a very special award. It's only given to people who have shown extra special courage in the face of the enemy."

"But Baz did show extra special courage in the face of the enemy!" insisted Rosie.

"Yeah, Baz was really brave after he'd been captured," said the Professor.

Georgie agreed.

"You should have seen the way he struggled to get free. He was wriggling and kicking his legs so much that they had a job to keep hold of him."

"And it was Baz who poked that stick into the wheel of PC Poynter's bike just as Bullivant was trying to escape on it," I pointed out.

"Yeah," laughed Jimmy. "He made Bullivant go flying right over the top of the handlebars."

"I think we should give Baz an Order of St. George," Beth told her brother.

There was a long pause.

"Alright then," agreed Michael grumpily, "you can give him the Order of St. George if you want to!"

From the grudging expression on Michael's face and the reluctant way in which he agreed, it was clear that our leader was far from convinced that Baz was deserving of this special honour. But in view of everybody else's support for Baz, Michael had been forced to agree that our little lance-corporal should be added to the roll of honour on the Balaclava Cup. The Professor and Charlie agreed to manufacture another Order of St. George medal, and the Professor said he would write out Baz's name in his very best handwriting so that it could be stuck underneath mine onto the side of the Balaclava Cup. A special presentation ceremony in honour of Baz was planned for first thing on Saturday morning.

"I've had a great idea," exclaimed Rosie unexpectedly.

Everyone turned and looked at her.

"The British army has lots of regimental bands. Our brigade ought to have its very own military band. We're a bit like a regiment because we've got a colonel in charge of us and we've got some regimental silver. If we formed a band we could march through the village playing our instruments whenever we've got something special to celebrate."

Everyone agreed that a Balaclava Brigade Military Band was an excellent idea. "We've got loads of instruments," I observed.

"Yeah, we've got tins that we could use as drums," argued Charlie.

"And there's my brass hunting horn that I bought at the Jumble Sale," said Georgie.

"I've got that gong that I bought at the Baptist Chapel," added Beth. "I knew it would be useful."

"I could use my bird-scarer rattle," said the Professor.

"And I've got that little bell that I bought for a penny," added Robbie.

"What about some trumpets?" asked Rosie. "Military bands always have trumpets"

"We ain't usin' rolled up newspapers like we did last time," vowed Baz.

"We could go to Brown's scrap field and look for some bits of tube or pieces of pipe from the old cars," suggested Charlie. "They would make super trumpets."

"That's a good idea," said Jimmy.

"A military band always has a chap marching at the front," advised Rosie. "He's called a drum major. He carries a long stick and he twirls it and throws it into the air as the band marches. Colonel Michael could be our drum major."

Up to that point Michael had been remarkably quiet and disinterested. However, the prospect of being the drum major had suddenly brought him to life.

"We could celebrate Archie Fraser leaving Stretton on Saturday morning," stated our colonel enthusiastically.

"And our victory over 'Mad Bull' Bullivant," said Robbie with a loud snuffle.

Everyone was very excited about the prospect of forming our very own Balaclava Brigade Military Band. Jimmy and Charlie went off to search Brown's scrap field for suitable trumpets. Michael hurried away to practise twirling his drum major's baton. The rest of the company began to rehearse on their various instruments, most of which had been purchased at the Baptist Chapel Jumble Sale. But in the confined space of our headquarters the noise was deafening and far from musical, so I hurried outside and climbed to our look-out post to get away from it all.

Chapter 38

Archie Leaves Stretton

Saturday morning arrived and the brigade assembled inside our HQ. On the table in front of us the Professor laid out the recently manufactured Order of St. George and the label bearing Baz's name.

"Captain Tommy, you can give Lance-corporal Baz his medal, because I didn't actually see what he did," said our colonel, who clearly did not want to have anything to do with this presentation.

"Where is Baz?" asked the Professor. "He's not here yet."

"I'll go and look for him," I said. "We need to give him his medal quickly because we don't want to miss Archie Fraser and his family leaving Stretton."

I walked round to the main road, followed by the others. I glanced up and down the street. Along by the Baptist chapel I could see Baz bending over and peering through the metal railings which surrounded the chapel grounds.

"Look there he is," I said, pointing up the road.

"Baz!" yelled Charlie.

He took no notice. Others began to shout his name but he simply ignored everyone.

"What's he doing?" asked the Professor.

"I don't know but we'd better go and see," said Georgie.

We raced along the pavement, shouting Baz's name as we ran. Still Baz took no notice as we approached. His head was poking through the railings and he seemed to be staring intently at something in the grass inside the chapel grounds. What could he be looking at?

"What are you doing, Baz?" asked Georgie.

"Lookin' at that shiny thing in the grass," Baz replied.

"We've been calling you! Why didn't you look at us?" demanded Michael with a definite edge to his voice.

"I couldn't," Baz replied. "'cus I've got me 'ead stuck in these railin's and I can't get it out."

"How long have you been there like that?" I asked.

"I've bin 'ere for ages," answered Baz. "I were out early this morning 'cus I knew I were goin' to get me medal."

"How did you get your head stuck in there?" I inquired.

"Well, I seen this shiny thing in the grass and I thought it were half-a-crown, so I squeezed me 'ead through the bars to 'ave a good look, but it weren't money. When I tried to get me 'ead out it were stuck."

"Don't worry Baz. We'll soon get you out of there," the Professor assured him.

Georgie was told to go inside the railings to push on Baz's forehead while Michael and I tugged on his body from the other side of the fence. We pushed and tugged until Baz screamed out in pain.

"It's no good," said Michael as he stood up straight. "We're never going to get him out like that. His ears are in the way."

"Let's chop them off then," chuckled Charlie.

"Get off! You ain't choppin' me ears off," Baz yelled. "You've already chopped all me 'air off," and he made another vain attempt to free his head.

"He hardly ever listens to anything that's said to him now," said Jimmy. "Without any ears he'd never hear anything."

Old Mrs. Jenks came hobbling along the pavement on her way to the shop. She stopped and peered over the top of her glasses at the strange sight of Baz bending forward with his head pushed through the chapel railings.

"What's he looking at?" she sputtered through her false teeth.

"He ain't looking at anything," replied Robbie. "He's got his head stuck."

"How on earth did he get his head stuck in there?" she asked.

Old Mr. Bickerstaff, with bronzed face and hollow cheeks, shuffled across the road from his cottage opposite, and stood leaning on his walking stick, gawping at the unfortunate little lad.

"That's a fine pickle he's got himself into," he commented, shaking his head in disbelief.

A number of local people living nearby either pulled aside their net curtains to see what was happening or stood at their open doors to watch. Several excited young children came running along the pavement to enjoy this unusual village spectacle. A man, riding by on his bike with his trouser legs tucked into his bulging socks, interrupted his journey to see what was happening. On seeing a large crowd gathering outside the chapel, a passing van driver also stopped to investigate, as did an army sergeant driving past in a huge lorry. When the army vehicle pulled up with a jolt a squad of two dozen soldiers in full battle dress emerged from the back, complete with helmets, rifles and packs on their backs. Eventually such a large crowd had gathered that it was spilling into the road.

"You'll need a big sledge hammer to bash those railings apart," remarked the man with the bike.

"You can't do that!" interrupted Mr. Bickerstaff, "You might hit the poor little kid on the 'ead."

"It might knock some sense into him," mumbled Michael under his breath.

"You might manage to get his head out of there by putting some butter or lard on his ears to make his head slippery," said the van driver.

"Don't be so silly!" spluttered Grandma Jenks. "You can't use butter or lard. There's a war on, and they're rationed."

"Go into that garage and ask for some car grease to rub over his ears," suggested the sergeant in charge of the army lorry. "With lots of grease on the side of his head we might be able to get him free."

Baz just stood there motionless and silent, his head protruding through the railings and his hands gripping the iron bars tightly. He looked like a wrongdoer from a distant age who had been condemned to stand in the pillory as a punishment for his villainous behaviour.

The Professor went off to Brown's garage to ask for a little vehicle grease, and he soon returned with a small round tin which was half full of thick slippery greenish-black lubricant. This was spread liberally over Baz's ears and both sides of his head. Some of the soldiers were ordered to pull on the bar beside Baz's right ear, while others were told to tug on the bar next to his left ear. We pushed both Baz's ears as close to his head as we could, and the army sergeant gave a sharp tug on our little lance-corporal's waist. Suddenly Baz's head slipped from between the bars, causing him and the sergeant to tumble backwards onto the pavement. The watching crowd erupted into a noisy bout of cheering and clapping, as if they had been watching a summer show on the end of a pier at the seaside.

"Are you alright?" asked the sergeant, staring into Baz's face.

"You what?" asked Baz, peering at him blankly.

"Are you alright now?" the sergeant yelled more loudly.

"I can't 'ear you," yelled Baz. "I've got this stuff in both me ear'oles."

Soon the man on the bike, the van driver and the army lorry full of soldiers were on their way again. Mrs. Jenks toddled off towards the shop, Mr. Bickerstaff hobbled back across the road towards his cottage, and the rest of the crowd dispersed to go about their usual business. On the opposite side of the road cottage doors slammed shut and net curtains fell back into place. The excitement was over. The Professor returned the tin of grease to Mr. Brown at the garage, and soon we were heading for our headquarters to present Baz with his Order of St. George for Valour.

Taking great care to avoid any contact with the large lumps of grease which were still clinging to his ears and both sides of his face, I had the pleasure of hanging the medal around Baz's neck. The Professor glued Baz's name to the side of the Balaclava Cup underneath my name. Baz was beside himself with joy. He stared proudly at the Brigade Cup and gently fondled the brigade's highest award which was now dangling from the string around his neck. This was his moment of true glory. At last Baz had been acclaimed as one of the heroes of the Balaclava Brigade. There were loud cheers as he stood before us, an enormous toothy grin stretching across his grease-smeared face and his wide eyes sparkling like giant blue gems.

"We've made two more medals," said Rosie. "There's one for Robbie, because he was very brave when he was driven away in the back of that lorry with a load of scrap metal. And there's also a medal for Tommy because he helped me back to HQ when I sprained my ankle in the woods. He also took the blame for me at school when I accidentally hit Archie Fraser on the head with that stone. Afterwards he had to go to Mr. Hardcastle's room, and so I think he was *really* brave."

Two Balaclava Gold Crosses, awards for exceptional courage in the line of duty, were placed on the top of the table. Robbie was delighted with his award and I was thrilled to be receiving another medal, especially since it was being awarded upon Rosie's recommendation.

Our medal award ceremony was suddenly cut short by a car horn sounding in the road at the front of the cottages. I scrambled up into our look-out post to see what was happening. A large black car had pulled up outside the front of Wilma Jones's cottage, and the driver kept pipping his horn impatiently.

"This must be the car that's come to take Archie and his family to Oakthorpe railway station," I thought.

We hid behind the wall of our headquarters and peered around the corner, our eyes fixed upon the Jones's scullery door. After a few minutes the door opened and Archie appeared, dragging a very large suitcase. His mother followed closely behind carrying an even larger case while Mavis, stumbling along on her high heels, brought up the rear carrying a couple of bags. We raced around to the front of Georgie's cottage and stood casually in a huddled group on the corner of Brick Fields Lane. We saw the Fraser family scramble into the car and we watched as the family luggage was loaded into the boot.

When the car pulled away in the direction of Oakthorpe Archie was sitting on the back seat beside the window nearest to us. As the car drove past, he stuck out his tongue and pulled faces at us. We chose to ignore him. After all, no matter how many faces he pulled, it was the Balaclava Brigade which had achieved the victory not him. We stared after the car as it went over the brow of the hill and disappeared from view. Then an enormous cheer went up. One of our main enemies had gone for good. He would cause our brigade no more trouble with his sneak-thieving, his lying and his tale-telling. In future, life would be so much happier at school, especially for Beth, Baz and Jimmy who had had been forced to put up with him in class.

"Now we are going to do something very special," stated our colonel. "Our military band is going to march through the village. Come on, chaps! Let's go and get our instruments."

Chapter 39

Victory Celebrations!

Soon we were lining up in Brick Fields Lane ready to begin our victory march. Colonel Michael stood in front of the band with a very long stick in one hand. In my left hand I carried a round tin which I was going to use as a drum, and in the other I held a piece of wood for a drumstick. Sergeant-Major Rosie was next, clutching her silver-coloured whistle. Sergeant Georgie was immediately behind her with his long hunting horn tucked under his arm. Immediately behind Sergeant Georgie was the Professor who was clasping his wooden bird-scarer firmly to his chest. Next in line were Corporal Charlie, Lance-Corporal Baz and Lance-Corporal Jimmy, each clutching a piece of metal piping, and behind them, gripping her dinner gong very tightly, was Private Beth. Bringing up the rear and holding his little tinkling bell between his thumb and forefinger was Private Robbie.

When our colonel gave the order, the band started to play, and as we did so we set off along the pavement in the direction of Oakthorpe. Colonel Michael was twirling and twisting his long stick at the head of the band like a proper military drum major. I was banging out a steady rhythm on my drum, and Sergeant-Major Rosie was blowing her shrill whistle as hard as her lungs would allow. Behind her, Sergeant Georgie was letting rip with loud blasts on his hunting horn, the end of which sounded as if it was only a couple of inches away from my right ear. The Professor continually twirled his rattle as if he was standing behind the goal at Oakthorpe Rovers' Football Ground. Every so often Private Beth gave her gong a hefty clout, while the trumpeters were doing their best to blow various tunes through their pieces of piping. Meanwhile, Private Robbie was ringing his tiny tinkling bell as if he were a terrier shaking a rat, but unfortunately his contribution to our musical performance was completely lost amidst the deafening din made by the rest of us.

On reaching the top of the hill which descends to Oakthorpe we halted and prepared to cross the road before marching back on the other side. We were most anxious that none of the inhabitants of Stretton should miss out on this wonderful musical experience. We were about to step off the pavement when an army truck, driven at breakneck speed, zoomed past us.

"He looks as if he's in a hurry," said Colonel Michael.

"It's those military police we saw the other day," cried Sergeant-Major Rosie.

"Yeah," agreed the Professor. "I saw the red tops to their caps."

"Oh great! Hitler's invasion is goin' to start soon," said Corporal Baz. "I'm ready for 'em."

We crossed over and continued with our musical celebration. As we marched and entertained the good folk of Stretton, we could not understand why doors and windows were being slammed shut, why an old lady in the street angrily shook her walking stick in our direction, why cats scurried away into entries and why dogs began to howl and bark as we approached their front gates. We were particularly careful to avoid marching in front of the Miner's Arms for fear that Norah Butterworth, the fearsome landlady of that establishment, might be lying in wait behind an open upstairs window with a large bucket of soapy water at the ready.

When we reached the Brinton end of our village another equally formidable creature was awaiting our arrival. As we approached its front garden hedge the ferocious German Shepherd Dog still attached to its long clanking chain came bounding up the path again and hurled itself feet first at the gate with a terrifying thud, its jaws snapping violently, and loud menacing throaty growls emerging from between its fearsome teeth. This huge beast took us so completely by surprise that our colonel tripped over the end of his long baton, Private Beth threw down her gong with a crash, Private Robbie's tinkling bell went clattering into the middle of the road, and the rest of us dropped our instruments, leapt several feet into the air and dashed away, shouting and squealing at the tops of our voices. Only Lance-Corporal Baz remained by the gate, where he stood staring menacingly at the vicious hound.

"Just 'cus you're one of 'itler's dogs it don't mean to say we're scared of you," he yelled, pointing his piece of metal piping at the vicious brute.

Having retired to a safe distance the rest of us recovered our composure and our instruments, and formed up into a line again, determined to complete our tuneful tour of the village.

Back inside our headquarters we were delighted with our victory celebration, although for some time afterwards I continued to experience a very loud ringing noise in both ears.

"That were brilliant," said Baz with a beaming smile. "I really henjoyed that."

"That was a great way to celebrate our victory over Archie Fraser," said Jimmy clenching both his fists.

"This village will be much better from now on," commented Georgie. "We've finally got rid of him!"

"Yes, and we shan't be bumping into 'Mad Bull' Bullivant for quite a while either," stated Michael. "Bullivant's dad was in the pub last night, and my dad heard him telling somebody that his son has got into so much trouble with PC Poynter that he's not going to let him go out for months."

"Great!" yelled Jimmy. "No more Archie Fraser and no more 'Mad Bull' Bullivant!"

"That's *two* great victories for the Balaclava Brigade!" cried the Professor.

"All for one and one for all!" shouted Baz, bouncing up and down on his seat.

"ALL FOR ONE AND ONE FOR ALL!" the rest of us bawled at the tops of our voices.

"But we shall still have to be careful!" said Rosie. "There's still that horrible Scarface. We'll have to make sure we keep out of his way."

"And we might bump into that Ginger gorilla in the woods as well!" added the Professor.

"Ginger gorilla!" yelled Baz. "You lot said that there ain't no such things as gorillas in our woods. I ain't goin' in them woods if there's a ginger gorilla in there. I don't like gorillas 'cus they're great big hairy things that can pick you up and squeeze you to death."

We all stared at Baz. His eyes were wide and staring, and his mouth was drooping open.

"Don't worry, Baz," giggled Charlie. "A gorilla would never hurt *you*. He'd think that you were a tiny baby gorilla that needed looking after."

Everybody lay back in their seats and laughed uproariously.

Although I laughed with the rest of my friends, mention of Scarface and Ginger had made me feel extremely nervous. I remembered how Scarface had nearly caught me in Brinton churchyard. I could still picture his hideous face as he bent down and peered into the slate tomb where I was hiding. Who were these two thugs, where had they come from and what were they doing in Brinton? The last thing I wanted to happen was to bump into that pair again.

Two days later we were in the pub square playing football. Baz had just thudded the ball against the pub wall for the umpteenth time, when an upstairs window above us rattled up and Nora Butterworth leaned out.

"Clear off!" she shrieked. "Go and play somewhere else. You lot are getting on my nerves!"

We stopped playing and I picked up the ball.

"Let's go and play in Blore's field," suggested Georgie.

"No, the grass is too long there," said the Professor.

"And all them black and white cows are there as well," mumbled young Robbie.

As we could not think of a suitable place to finish our game of football we strolled towards the main road, heading for our brigade headquarters. As we ambled slowly towards the edge of the square I was suddenly aware of heavy footsteps running along the pavement. Whoever these people were they seemed to be in a tremendous hurry. Then two huge figures careered around the corner of the pub into the square. My heart sank to the soles of my shoes. It was Scarface and Ginger and they were heading straight for us. I could not believe our bad luck!

"Quick! Run!" I yelled, for I was determined to escape. I was already sprinting across the square towards the lane which led to Blore's Farm and the Tunnel Top.

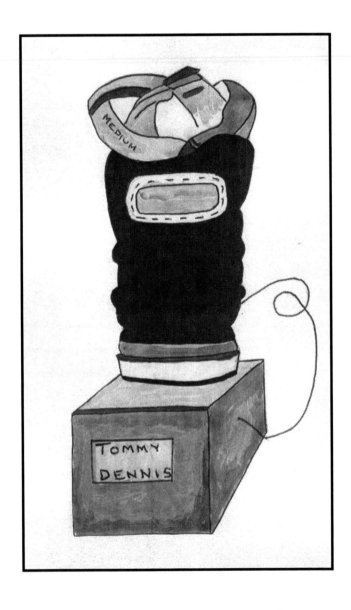

Chapter 40

Victory at Last

Those two brutes had taken us completely by surprise, for they seemed to have appeared from nowhere. As I tore across the square and into the lane I could hear their huge boots pounding the ground behind me. I knew that they were coming after me, and they certainly seemed to be catching me up. At any minute I expected to feel a gigantic pair of hands grab me from behind.

Then to my total amazement I could see that Scarface was dashing straight past me. It was not long before Ginger also overtook me, and both of them were now racing down the lane like Olympic sprinters. I stopped running and looked around. The other members of the brigade were also standing still, staring after Scarface and Ginger as they hared down the hill towards Blore's Farm. I turned around again and stared after the pair of thugs as they dashed away as if their lives depended on it. What on earth was happening?

Then something incredibly unexpected and dramatic happened. I heard the roar of an engine and a screeching of tyres behind me. I spun around to see a small khaki-coloured truck careering around the corner into the pub square. After a few seconds I realised that it was the British army truck which we had seen a couple of days earlier. I stared in bewilderment as it accelerated across the square in a cloud of dust and hurtled past me into the lane. Down the hill it sped and when it finally skidded to a halt four burly military policemen leapt out, for I could see the red tops on their peaked caps, and they had white arm bands on their sleeves.

"Crikey!" I heard Rosie call out. "It's those red caps."

Before I had chance to take in what was happening, the military policemen had grabbed hold of Scarface and Ginger, and bundled them into the back of the truck.

We could not believe what had happened. It seemed like a miracle! But why were a group of military policemen taking Scarface and Ginger away? What had these two scruffy individuals done? We ran down the lane to the vehicle and peered into the back of it. The two thugs were sitting hunched up between two of the red caps. For the first time those vicious brutes looked anything but threatening, for there was a definite look of resignation and defeat on their faces.

The driver of the truck walked along the side of his vehicle, and clambered into the driving seat. I could see that he had a lance-corporal's stripe on his tunic. We clustered around the vehicle, our eyes riveted upon the driver as he started the engine.

"I'm a lance-corporal," shouted Baz, peering through the open window. "What are you goin' to do with 'em?"

"We're taking them away for questioning," the driver answered.

"Why's that?" asked Georgie.

"They're deserters from the army," replied the driver. "They had their call-up papers to join the army a couple of months ago, but I'm afraid they've been very naughty lads."

"My dad's a sergeant-major in the army," said Rosie. "What have those two done?"

"They attacked their drill sergeant, and then decided to run away from their training camp. They've been absent without leave for the last three weeks. We had information that they'd come to Brinton and were living rough in this area. The local policeman told us that he'd seen them around here with a lad called Bullivant. We found out they were living in a den in the woods, and that Bullivant was stealing food for them. Unfortunately when the local bobby took us to the den there was nobody there. We've been scouring this area for several days looking for these two bright beauties."

"How did you know they'd come to our village today?" asked the Professor.

"Well, we came across them quite by accident. We were driving along this road towards Stretton, and we spotted them walking towards the pub. Unfortunately they saw us first and that's when they started to run."

"I'm glad you've copped them," said little Robbie with a mighty sniff.

"Well, I ain't scared of 'em," said Baz. "I'm a lance-corporal and I'm a hexpert commando."

We stood and watched as the driver revved up his engine, turned his vehicle around, and sped away, the wheels of his truck spinning in a cloud of dirt. Then it shot up the lane and zoomed out of the square, before finally roaring away in the direction of Oakthorpe. We stood for a few moments, stunned by the speed with which everything had occurred.

"I can't believe what's just happened!" said the Professor.

"Nor me!" yelled Rosie. "We've been saved by some British army red caps! Just wait 'til my dad hears about this!"

"What will happen to Scarface and Ginger now?" asked Robbie.

"If they've attacked their sergeant and then gone absent without leave they'll be locked up for quite a long time," replied Rosie.

"I reckon they deserve everything that's coming to them," I muttered.

"They were really horrible," said Beth

"Yeah, I'm glad to see the back of them," gasped Georgie.

"And me!" said Michael. "Well, there's one good thing. We shall never have to worry about them, ever again."

Everyone breathed a sigh of relief, and then a deafening cheer filled the air.

We returned to our HQ, scarcely able to believe our good fortune. We were in excellent spirits, and we had every reason to be so. We had cleverly outwitted our two main enemies – sneaky troublesome Archie Fraser and that vicious bully, 'Mad Bull' Bullivant. We were even more delighted that a group of British Army red caps had finally relieved us of Bullivant's terrifying henchmen.

"From now on we shall be able to concentrate on drawing up the plans to guard our village against Hitler's soldiers when they land," announced Colonel Michael.

"As long as we don't attack our own Home Guard blokes by mistake," giggled Corporal Charlie.

"But we dain't get the blame for that, did we?" said Lance-Corporal Baz with a grin.

We all lay back on our straw-filled seats, laughing and giggling. We were feeling extremely relieved and very proud of ourselves. Although the ambush in Stretton Woods had not gone quite according to plan, we felt that the Balaclava Brigade had proved itself to be a first rate military company, able to undertake secret undercover operations, stage ambushes and employ guerrilla tactics.

We were confident that we would be able to play our part in defending our village against invading German soldiers, and we would not flinch from our duty. We would face our foes with the utmost courage and daring, just like true British soldiers. After all, our record as a military unit spoke for itself. Against all the odds, the Balaclava Brigade had defeated its enemies and, with just a little help from our comrades in the British army, we had finally emerged victorious!

Printed in the United Kingdom by
Lightning Source UK Ltd., Milton Keynes
137696UK00001B/1/P